# The Enlightenment of INFERON

# THE ENLIGHTENMENT OF INFERON

Steve Denton

authorHOUSE®

*AuthorHouse™*
*1663 Liberty Drive*
*Bloomington, IN 47403*
*www.authorhouse.com*
*Phone: 1-800-839-8640*

*Published by AuthorHouse    05/23/2012*

*ISBN: 978-1-4772-1112-0 (sc)*
*ISBN: 978-1-4772-1111-3 (hc)*
*ISBN: 978-1-4772-1110-6 (e)*

*Library of Congress Control Number: 2012909399*

*For: My family*

# CONTENTS

# PREFACE

It was a cold winter morning with intermittent snow showers during the night. At the time, I worked in the hybrid microelectronics department for a high tech company in Beaverton, Oregon. Arriving more than two hours before my colleagues, I used the quiet time to concentrate on a piece of test evaluation software I was writing. A large pyramid shaped skylight over my desk provided a view into the early morning darkness above. After about an hour of writing computer code, I leaned back in my chair to rest my eyes from the green monochrome display, and to think. As I looked up into the darkness, a fresh snow shower began falling upon the glass. In the lights, the flakes looked a bit like stars passing by a starship on a science fiction movie. My mind began to wander away from component life test software, and toward an idea I'd been thinking about for a while.

Inspiration often comes when it's least expected, and that was the case that morning. On impulse, I returned to the computer and spent about fifteen minutes writing what I called a "Starspondence message" to a friend on mine living in Colorado. In those days, email was still in its infancy, and neither of us had internet access. I finished the note and sent it to him via regular mail the following day. The name of the vessel in the message, "Inferon," was a derivative of a name "Interferon," which was a drug used for a variety of treatments including multiple sclerosis, autoimmune disorders, many cancers, and in Russia, even the flu. I thought the name fit well since the Inferon's purpose was to fight a disease as well . . . A disease called tyranny.

Even though the first message, and all that followed, didn't include the premise of The Enlightenment of Inferon as it appears in this work, the basic kernel was still there. There was a powerful interstellar vessel called the "Inferon," a self-aware cybernetic computer system with a problem, and a federation of worlds it was designed to defend. The following is an exact copy of that twenty-seven year old message:

\*\*\*\*\*\*\*\*\*\*\*\*\*\*\*\*\*\*\*\*\*\*\*\*\*\*\*\*\*\*\*\*\*\*\*\*\*\*\*\*\*\*\*\*\*\*\*\*\*\*\*\*\*\*\*\*\*\*\*\*\*\*\*\*\*\*\*\*\*\*\*\*\*\*\*\*\*\*\*\*\*

# United federation of Starships

\*\*\*\*\*\*\*\*\*\*\*\*\*\*\*\*\*\*\*\*\*\*\*\*\*\*\*\*\*\*\*\*\*\*\*\*\*\*\*\*\*\*\*\*\*\*\*\*\*\*\*\*\*\*\*\*\*\*\*\*\*\*\*\*\*\*\*\*\*\*\*\*\*\*\*\*\*\*\*\*\*

### \*\*\* Urgent Message \*\*\*

To: Adm. M. H2OST
United Federation Starship Command

From: Capt. Steve
Cdr. UFS Inferon

Subject: Whispership Cybernetic Intelligence

The cybernetic intelligence system incorporated into the intergalactic whispership control and navigation equipment needs to be evaluated as soon as possible. This intelligent system functions correctly for all aspects of ship defense, scanning, data processing, hyperdrive unit controls, system maintenance, etc. However, there is a very serious problem relating to the whispership control sequences during inter-dimensional transfer.

The cybernetic system tell me that it experiences momentary lapses of memory and/or loss of orientation at the moment of transfer into the normal space continuum from the 0 dim continuum necessary for intergalactic travel. I have tested this response from the cyber by making some short (3 to 5 light year) jumps into relatively low mass density areas. During the tests, I noted a sudden but short shuddering as the ship re-emerged into the 3 dim continuum. This shuddering is confirmation of the cybernetic systems momentary confusion, and the resulting sudden reorientation of the ship.

It is absolutely imperative that this problem be resolved as soon as possible since it could result in a non-avertable collision with a star or other object result in disaster for my ship and myself as well as any planet or star within 1 to 1.5 parsecs in any direction of the blast.

Please schedule a therapy and repair program for my cybernetic equipment at the main star base in star cluster Orion. I estimate arrival at the base in 2 to 3 days using short calculated jumps of less than three light years to be safe. I cannot risk a single 1500 light year jump at this time.

With urgent sincerity
Capt. Steve
United Federation Starship Inferon.

**********************************************************************************

To my surprise, my friend sent back a reply. Over the years, we exchanged numerous Starspondence messages, which I still have in a file today. Many weren't very well written, and none followed a defined outline, but they were nonetheless fun to write. From time to time, they also included cleverly hidden information. One of the more obvious examples is shown below. When I planned to visit my friend where he lived in Colorado, he sent a Starspondence message that, hidden within the context of the story, included instructions on how to get to his place. The following is an excerpt from his message:

> ". . . The next possible opening for that length of repair time is Aenuj or maybe even Tsugua. With the proper coordinates and time, you should be able to make the jump to here in a single bound. The following are the vectors with which you are to travel in order to penetrate our outer shield without vaporizing into thin space. Remember that your co-pilot will not be used to this type of jump, so be prepared to handle the re-entry yourself. V112S, V112, V298, V520, V6, V4, V4. Squak 118.3 upon entry to LM, CO. For final approach instructions, squak 112.8. Good trip."

Translated, he was telling me that I should plan on visiting him in June or August, and that I should be able to make the trip without an overnight stay (non-stop). Furthermore, my friend Brian who would be traveling with me shouldn't be counted on to help drive (he did in fact sleep most of the trip). The "V" numbers are aviation victor airways that an airplane can use to navigate from Portland, Oregon to Longmont, Colorado. Those victor airways pass roughly over the cities of The Dalles,

Baker City, Boise, Twin falls, Rock Springs, and Cheyenne, the very cities I'd pass through on the way there in a car. Quite clever, I thought. The 118.3 and 112.8 are frequencies he probably made up for the Longmont, Colorado airport.

With fifteen years of high tech experience, college, twenty more years as a professional aviator, and several technical training manuals under my belt, I decided to apply the expertise and experience I have to writing a science fiction novel. About two years ago, I got serious about writing the story of the United Federation Vessel Inferon and its roll in the federation of worlds. Some locations such as Enif, Phi-1 Orionis, Earth (of course), and a couple others are actual celestial bodies. Others are imaginative constructs. The volume of space encompassing the federation and the number of habitable systems existing within in such a volume fit with the current observation of extra solar planets, and statistical probability. Additionally, the chapter called "The science of supernova" details the general series of events leading up to a supernova as we know it today.

The story of the federation, and the Inferon, represent the conflict between pure technology and something that can't be written into the software of a computer system. Simply put, in the purely physical world dominated by technology, two plus two can never be anything but four. However, in the spiritual and emotional world, two plus two must equal anything but four. Only by embracing both can a totality of understanding be realized. As the United Federation of Worlds grows to encompass thousands of worlds, and the "Iclass" vessels are developed to assist an existing defense system, a problem that plagues all advanced civilizations emerges . . . One that can't be solved within the context of any software algorithm.

Capt Steven R Denton

*"The totality of the universe cannot be discerned through mortal eyes alone."*

# PROLOGUE

## CHILDREN OF THE SKY

*"Then we shall . . . be able to take part in the discussion of the
question of why it is that we and the universe exist. If we find
the answer to that, it would be the ultimate triumph of human
reason—for then we would know the mind of God."*
*Stephen Hawking*

It is a truth as old as recorded history itself. Civilizations regardless of
origin or circumstance eventually grapple with others for resources, room
to grow, and control as their populations expand from villages to nations
to empires. Changes in addition to population growth occur too. These
include but are not limited to the slow but steady erosion of spiritual
ideology as the sciences begin to explain things previously accepted on
faith alone. Government and social laws eventually replace the rule of tribal
elders to avoid anarchy and chaos in larger populations. Armed military
powers become necessary to enforce the law upon those who reject it and
to protect the community from foreign interference or invasion. When
technology advances enough to provide travel between the stars, the
people of one world inevitably meet the people of others. The probability
of conflict and the complexity of cooperation will grow with each new
contact. How they cooperate as an interstellar community, the law they
collectively choose to respect, and the tools they use to enforce those laws
ultimately affect the fate of them all, sometimes in unexpected ways.

The United Federation of Worlds was a vast consortium of independent
worlds that grappled with all of those issues. Technologically advanced
and protected by a powerful military machine, its volume spread across
thousands of light years and encompassed many worlds. All members

cooperated with one another as civilized worlds and provided funding and support for the huge military. In exchange, the United Federation government promised protection from outside interference, resolved internal disputes, and enforced trade agreements and civil rights laws established between its members.

Nevertheless, as the federation grew to encompass more than 5000 worlds and tens of thousands of outposts spread out over a volume more than 20,000 light years across, a new problem emerged. The federation military despite its size was sometimes too slow to respond effectively. Certain conflicts by their nature required a fast response to settle a dispute or protect a member world. During high council meetings, the military eventually came under scrutiny because of this perceived weakness. Some representatives argued that even though the military was well outfitted, it had to work toward continuous improvement in the area of response time. However, like all big government, action was frequently mired by seemingly endless debate. It was inevitable that something dreadful would finally force the federation into action. It did. A terrible and bloody assault upon the Eucleade world by a non-federation race of warriors cost millions of lives before the military arrived to fight off a fierce and relentless enemy. News of the conflict caused uproar among federation representatives who demanded action during the following federal government high council meetings that convened on the capitol world of Urianaz. The overwhelming complaint was that a solution had to be found. If one was not, some even threatened to secede from the federation union and develop their own smaller federations that could more effectively protect their local interests.

It was during those meeting that an idea was proposed to enhance military response time and restore stability. The United Federation of Worlds Strategic Sciences Council suggested that a dedicated first line of defense device be developed. Its purpose would be to arrive quickly and bring to bear the formidable power necessary to deter or at least slow down acts of aggression in advance of federal fleet resources. When the idea was accepted, all worlds within the federation were invited to participate with technology and funding to support it. More than five hundred of them eventually participated in the research and development of the machines. There would be three.

It took years to settle upon a specific set of specifications. Stability and a consistent unerring adherence to the goals and desires of the United

Federation of Worlds would be of paramount importance. Therefore, the crews would be genetically modified to accommodate a lifetime service aboard the vessels. Their computer systems would be the most advanced cybernetic devices ever built. Complex enough to be considered sentient "self-aware" members of the crew. The vessels would include the latest technologies available making them the single most powerful devices ever devised. Such power also brought concern among certain members who added to the discussion and debate that such power could, if used the wrong way become an even greater enemy than those they already had. In response to such concerns, the list of specifications would also include infallible remote destruct systems to prevent such an occurrence. In addition, a similar cybernetic intelligent system would be located at the central command complex on Urianaz. It and the federation council would be in constant communication with each of the vessels. No decision or action of any significance would be accomplished without federation consent.

When the discussions ended, the task of making an objective plan into functional reality fell to the scientists, engineers, and builders. Nearly seventy years later, the first vessel launched from a huge hangar orbiting over the member world of Hermaptor. After its departure, member worlds watched the United Federation Vessel Westix carefully as it performed its duty. The initial anxiety some felt regarding such power gave way to pride and appreciation as the vessel and its crew performed with distinction. It would be more than sixty more years before the second and even more capable vessel launched from a subterranean silo on a moon orbiting the planet Enif. The UFV Sagin was more than six miles long and beautiful in both form and function. Its crew consisted of more than one hundred genetically modified Urinanazain beings. Its cybernetic intelligent mental direct interconnect system held the added advantage of pseudo telepathic communications with certain leading members of its crew. This was accomplished using beta wave modulators located over certain duty stations that could transmit and receive "active thought" from the brain of the being under the interface. It was affectionately nicknamed CIMDI by its crew. Together with the UFV Westix they represented the most brilliant achievement of modern science.

However, the most impressive was yet to come. The day the UFV Sagin launched from Enif to begin its service to the federation, the facility to house project Inferon was just beginning on a small moon orbiting the planet Earth. Similar in design to the one used to build the UFV Sagin, it included a city of assembly stations, science labs, factories, and living facilities to accommodate tens of thousands of scientists, engineers, and workers. The roof of the cavern itself was three miles below the surface. At five miles high, eight miles wide, and twelve miles long it was one of the biggest excavation projects of its time! One end opened along the steep inside wall of a crater near the lunar south pole called the Atican Basin. Around the opening, they constructed one of the largest containment fields of its time. Simply stabilizing and sealing the rest of the rock within the cavern to support a breathable atmosphere for those who would build the vessel took months.

By the time the Inferon's polished seven mile long polydiametic hull was formed the children were about to be "born." Prior to conception the modified human DNA was purged of all known errors to enhance the mental propensity for such an important, complex, and long term service. Adolescence would last into their thirties, young adulthood into their sixties, and old age beyond seven hundred! Seventy of the best of them would crew the great vessel. Fifteen alternates would remain at the facility to become the statistical "control group" the genetic and behavioral scientists would monitor. These members would not sit idle though. With the same abilities as their crewmates, these highly intelligent people would make significant contributions to science and knowledge, and earn a respected place in the program without ever stepping foot on the vessel itself. The birthing facility where the renowned team of genetic scientists, doctors, nurses, and technicians lead by Dr. Hab and Dr. Blic worked adjoined the huge cavern alongside many other facilities there.

The computer monitoring system connected to each of the uterine systems used for extracorporeal gestation confirmed they were ready. The first baby emerged from the fluid world of the artificial womb and breathed his first breath in the hands of the genetic genius, Dr. Hab himself.

"This one is to be the captain," Dr. Hab said smiling to his colleagues.

"He will be called Marc in honor of his donors Marelius Arthus and Reccia Claruv." Shortly after birth he was checked for evidence of abnormality, verified to be genetically sound, and tested for body and brain activity. Had any of these shown abnormality, a "leader alternate" would replace him. Following within a couple hours of his removal from the uterine system, a female was born. She would be the Navigation Specialist named Inia. The future Weapons Specialist Seale, Communications Specialist Jiin, Science Specialist Mec, and the remaining members of the crew and alternates totaling 85 beings would all follow shortly thereafter.

The cybernetic system was built and installed shortly after the hull was formed. With the last of the self-correcting neuropathic algorithms installed, the cybernetic system was ready. Upon activation the fantastically complex interplay between millions of neural net subroutines, a database containing almost all known knowledge, and the most complex physical core processor ever built began. It joined, intertwined, synchronized, and melded together into a single entity, becoming self-aware one hour, thirty-three minutes, and eleven seconds after activation. The synthetic life form called CIMDI was born. To distinguish the Inferon CIMDI from that of the UFV Sagin they would be referred to as CIMDI-i and CIMDI-s respectively. Years of detailed cognitive behavioral analysis and scenario-based simulations were performed upon CIMDI as it too was prepared for centuries of service to the federation. Every moment and every action scrutinized to the finest detail. As the vessel's core processor the cybernetic intelligent system began suggesting design modifications to enhance performance. By controlling mechanized androids, it participated with the construction of many subsystems within the vessel. One of them was a formidable matter-energy conversion complex. The computer claimed it would extend the life of the machine by facilitating the ability to fabricate updated systems or replace aging or damaged components. Another was the installation of additional beta wave modulators at stations other than the command bridge so it could communicate mentally with more members of the crew. This would be especially useful if a larger number of them chose to visit a planet surface or other vessel via the hypercybergenic form generators. The HCG form generators as they were commonly called created a physical duplicate of the user at a remote location via a matter transporter system. The beta wave modulators then "transferred" their active thought to the form allowing the user to experience all five senses through it as if they were physically present at its location. Even activities such as eating and drinking were available through them. To protect the user from possible mental trauma, the sensation of pain or death was automatically blocked if the form were to become damaged or destroyed. These devices represented a significant advancement over older style transporter systems and were incorporated as requested.

The children destined to protect life among the stars were full of life themselves. Happy and well adjusted they laughed, played, learned, and grew. The colorful joy of childhood life inside the learning and development center was a stark contrast to the barren silence of the lifeless lunar surface above. As young children, they played simple games and bonded with the cognitive and behavioral development specialists they thought of as "parents." Such interaction was essential to the development of their young brains. They often communicated with the computer aboard the vessel and learned to think of it as one of them. In addition, they could see the vessel they would inhabit through the transparent beryllium windows of the learning center. They enjoyed outside experiences too. After learning to use the HCG form generators in the facility, they visited the construction area and "traveled" to earth. Visits outside the construction facility were somewhat frustrating because of the two and a half second delay in three-dimensional communications (3com) when they visited earth. The increasing delay with distance prohibited HCG usage further than that until the zero dimensional communications system (or Zcom for short) was activated. When the instantaneous transmission of the Zcom system became available, they were able to experience many worlds within the federation. Through it, they learned to appreciate the people and places they would spend their lives protecting.

The children grew into 35-year-old adolescents. Even though their education and training was organized and structured to minute detail, they were still human. As such, they developed emotional desires in the areas of social interaction and sexuality that normal people did during that time in their lives. Knowing such interaction could not be suppressed by genetic modification without destroying the person, the behavioral specialists and teachers educated them in these areas as well. Nevertheless, the complexities it would present during their lifetime cohabitation and mission meant that interaction on a personal physical level with one another would not be allowed. Instead, the HCG system included, in addition to its primary function, a sizable database of human forms that would provide surrogates to meet the physical contact requirements for each of the crew.

They reached late adolescents as the giant normal space (NS) and zero space (ZS) engines were installed. Thirty huge energy conduits, each more than a mile and a half long harnessed and focused the power of quark-gluon plasma for propulsion. Its purple-blue luminance bathed the propulsion enclosure with its hypnotizing glow as the great engines were charged for the first time.

In the learning center, each future crew person trained within their specific area of expertise using a wide variety of scenarios and complex full function simulators. Even at an early age the boy named Marc clearly demonstrated his ability make correct decisions under the pressure of complex simulations, and easily demonstrated his ability to lead his crew. Inia, especially gifted in spatial orientation skills, eventually scored higher than the professors who designed the tests. Mec delved deeper into the scientific study and association of data into coherent knowledge than many scientists who were twice his age. The instructors watched and recorded every individual every second of his or her life. Every action was analyzed by a legion of behavioral scientists. About the time the weapon systems were incorporated, the crew was finishing extensive studies related to sociology, ethics, and military strategy. The huge vessel would carry a formidable array of weapon and defense systems. These included a mass to energy to anti-mass conversion system used to generate significant quantities of antimatter, and two plasma knife weapons capable of cutting a large ship completely in half! Additionally, plasma laser systems were installed along strategic areas of the outer hull allowing near limitless targeting coverage around the vessel. The harder than diamond polydiametic hull was protected by a complex multifaceted, multi-phased force field array. This array functioned as a dual-purpose system, both absorbing and deflecting energy as the situation required. Marc, Seale, and Siven in particular trained to use the CIMDI system to assess tactical displays, select and deploy suitable weapon systems, and target large numbers of simulated attack vessels simultaneously.

For more than fifty years, the members of the crew were educated and trained in preparation for their duty to the federation. Finally as young sixty-year-old adults the day came when they would enter the huge ship. The last direct contact with their teachers within the facility was followed by a traditional "preflight" inspection aboard small hovercraft in which the crew would inspect the vessel before the commissioning and boarding ceremony. Marc and several of his crew climbed aboard the first shuttle. The driver took them across the nearly pointed bow and down along one side to the plasma knife array and the antimatter deflection panels.

"It's beautiful." Marc said as they swept up and over part of the gleaming upper hull on their way toward the aft sections. Reaching the huge engine nacelles at the aft of the vessel they passed across the face of them before returning to the bow, and back to the shuttle-parking center. It would be the last time Marc or any of his crew would see the exterior of the ship with their own eyes. After returning to the conference center, the crew met with visiting federation dignitaries through windows to avoid the possibility of disease or contamination. Federation member worlds and their representatives at Urianaz viewed a customary christening ceremony live. Project Inferon became formally titled the United Federation Vessel INFERON on January 18, 4957 of the earth calendar. Marc officially became Captain Marc on that day. Inia received her commission as Navigation Specialist Inia, and Mec received his commission as Science Specialist Mec. All the others who would crew the vessel received their commissions that day too. The last detail of the formal celebration was to transport each of the crewmembers into the vessel. Once all of them were aboard and the huge vessel lifted from its assembly cradle, the multifaceted protection field generator would activate, preventing any further biological transfer in or out of the vessel.

Captain Marc entered the UFV Inferon first. He found himself standing near the physical core processor area located at the forward end of the huge propulsion systems enclosure. Rows of energy conduits pulsed with quark-gluon energy that cast a faint blue tint upon the otherwise pure white deck below his feet. A faint rumble sound filled the air. He remembered seeing this area in HCG form years ago while construction was underway. Assembly equipment, components waiting to be installed and busy service androids filled many of the empty spaces. Now the entire compartment was spotlessly clean. For the moment, and maybe the only moment ever, Captain Marc was the lone biological entity aboard the vessel. His thoughts were interrupted by the familiar and friendly voice of CIMDI over a hidden speaker.

The words, "Welcome aboard the UFV Inferon," echoed across the huge compartment.

"Thank you CIMDI," he replied.

Over the next few minutes all seventy of the crew transported to the floor of the cavernous propulsion compartment near the clear metal windows through which they could see the CIMDI system core array. Its columns and rows of processor units hung suspended in a clear fluid coolant. Each processor cube was connected on all sides by data conduits that glowed with a violet hue. Each member of the crew was required to step inside a circle where the beta wave modulator could connect them directly with CIMDI and verify their identity before they proceeded to their duty stations. Captain Marc stepped into the circle first.

He thought, *"I am Marc, Captain of the UFV Inferon."*

*"Hello Captain Marc, welcome aboard the Inferon. I am glad you are here. I am ready to serve the federation under your command,"* CIMDI replied as if it were a thought in his mind.

*"I am looking forward to us working together in the service of the federation as well,"* Captain Marc thought back.

A slight smile crossed his face as he completed the mental direct communication and stepped out of the circle.

Navigation Specialist Inia noticed and asked him about it.

"I am pleased that such technology is at our disposal, that's all," he replied.

"Oh, I saw your smile and became curious of your thoughts," Nav Specialist Inia admitted as she stepped into the circle.

*"Hello Navigation Specialist Inia. Welcome aboard the Inferon . . ."*

Each of the seventy people who would spend the remainder of their lives aboard the UFV Inferon took their turn identifying with CIMDI before entering transfer alcoves that transported them within the vessel to their assigned duty stations. Captain Marc entered one and transferred to the command bridge. Finding his place in the command chair near the center of the spacious bridge, he settled in and relaxed. The view from his seat included a clear and crisp visual of the inside of the construction cavern. The view was unobstructed, as if the vessel around the command bridge was transparent. He'd been there a thousand times before in the simulator. The others of his crew arrived and found their places as well. Captain Marc and his crew busied themselves with system tests and orientation as they prepared to move the great ship for the first time. When the appointed time neared, Captain Marc checked with each of his crew. Following that, he reported to the hangar crew that all primary system were checked and the UFV Inferon was ready for initial hover. After receiving word that all support personnel were clear, Captain Marc prepared to give the first order of his career. He turned to Nav Specialist Inia, "Lift us off the cradle, Z plus 1000 feet."

"Yes sir," she replied, turning to her navigation control console.

The huge vessel lifted from its cradle and hovered. The multifaceted protection field generator activated. From that point, the UFV Inferon was protected even from its makers. For two more days it remained stationary while they continued checking internal systems in preparation for departure. When it was time, Captain Marc communicated with the hangar controllers who reset the field strength of the containment field at the open end of the hangar cavern and cleared the UFV Inferon for departure. Upon Captain Marc's instruction, Navigation Specialist Inia moved the vessel slowly forward. The powerful containment field at the opening of the huge facility weakened just enough to allow the vessel to pass through it into the vacuum without letting the air within the facility escape. After clearing the opening, the UFV Inferon ascended slowly upward above the desolate gray floor of the Atican Basin. Lifting from the shadow of the crater rim its smooth surface gleamed in the bright light of earth's sun for the first time.

For the next three hundred years, the great federation vessels Westix, Sagin, and Inferon moved about federation space in the performance of their duty with nearly flawless integrity. During that time, several undesirable events that could have escalated into dreadful wars didn't. Just as designed, one or more of them would quickly arrive and settle the dispute. They effectively negotiated peaceful solutions, applied the correct measure of power to end conflicts, or provided support to federation military forces already involved. As their power became widely known, fewer and fewer aggressive incidents occurred within the federation. Members of the federation high council applauded the long deceased visionaries who recognized the need, and put into action these wonderful instruments of peace.

# CH 1

## THIRTEEN BILLION YEARS

*"Since wars begin in the minds of men, it is in the minds of men
that the defenses of peace must be constructed."*
*Unesco*

In the captains chair aboard the flagship Paquet Commander Iss took
a rare moment to relax. The exercises were over. The Paquet and its fleet
of support vessels completed yet another training mission where they
successfully located and eliminated several simulated rouge pirate frigates.
Once the assessment and debriefing of the exercise was complete and the
appropriate reports filed, they would move on to their next assignment.

Before he could let his mind wander too far from his duty as the ships
captain the information console chimed. He leaned a bit closer to the
device.

With a sigh he spoke, "accept transmission."

Moments later the new message appeared. He knew its general content
before he read it. His mind drifted for a moment to all that transpired to
put this message on his monitor. He knew changes as big as the ones sure
to come were a long time in the making, but now they were upon him.
He'd been apprehensive about his world joining the federation since the
first debate on the subject years ago. During the political process that
ensued, he attended numerous meetings on the subject of joining the
United Federation of Worlds and participated with both comment and
opinion for the record. His opinion differed from that of the political
leaders though. Their motivation centered on political and economic
matters. His was more concerned with preserving peace and defending his

world from the aggressive acts of others. As far as he was concerned, his world managed to remain free without any outside help.

Commander Iss's priorities formed early in his life. Having grown up with a father and a grandfather who were both generals in their time, Asun Iss adopted many of their attitudes and opinions at an early age. All through his time at the academy and the service to his world that followed, he believed simple adherence to a defined set of laws and the application of military strategies were enough. It wasn't as though politics were unknown or unimportant to him, in fact he understood them quite well. It was just that they were secondary to the greater value he found in practical and simple logic. Acts of aggression were just that, acts of aggression. No amount of political maneuvering would ever revive the dead or evaporate a single drop of spilled blood.

His "keep politics and emotion out of the mission objective" attitude had served him well through two wars, several military police actions, and numerous negotiations. As a result, a career that began as an inexperienced navigation lieutenant matured into that of the seasoned military commander who was now Lead Commander of the Anasec space defense contingent.

Nevertheless, his military point of view was only one of many. His government and his world had its own list. High on that list was the fact that over the last few decades several of the worlds Anasec traded with became members of the United Federation of Worlds. With their alliance came lopsided trade agreements and preferences resulting from higher taxes and tariffs on non-member worlds such as Anasec. It wasn't as though the federation intended to manipulate or pressure outside worlds like his into their coalition but the cost of doing business as a non member was nonetheless expensive.

Another factor they considered was the fact that the Anasec system was located on the fringe of a very large volume of space controlled by it. With federation worlds on one side and the vast unknown on the other Anasec finally made its choice. As Commander Iss prepared to read the transmission, his world was in the last stages of a lengthy and complex agreement. He couldn't quite put a finger on what it was that made him uneasy. *"After all the federation had no history of violence other than to defend itself. Maybe it was simply 'change' that made him feel that way,"* he thought. He trusted, no, he hoped the high council understood what they were doing. Because history was filled with examples of political decisions both good and bad. Unfortunately, the bad ones often tended to drag the military into senseless and bloody conflicts.

The transmission on his monitor was a response to questions the Anasec Central Government Council posed regarding the mysterious "superships" the federation claimed guaranteed peace. He'd heard rumors and unofficial reports regarding them but had never seen one, not even a holographic image of one. With them, the federation promised protection allegedly from any aggressor. Considering them from the standpoint of a career military mind Commander Iss wanted a copy of the report, not just to satisfy his curiosity but also to assess their military implication.

He reclined in his command chair scanning the stars through the windows. "*Peaceful,*" he thought. "*Quiet, just as it should be.*" Around the bridge, his command crew went about their duties. To his left were the scanning and science teams. To his right the weapon systems officers, communications, and environmental monitors. Just below his forward view were the navigation and tactical analysis crew. Beyond them, the transparent beryllium windows provided a magnificent view of space. The thousands of others busily doing their assigned tasks aboard his ship also crossed his mind. For a while, he could afford the luxury of some time to read the report. Eyeing the cup of purple liquid sitting on his console, he reached out and took it feeling its warmth with his three-fingered hand. Derf was a tasty beverage made from the fermented larvae of Derfenisa beetles. It had a mild aroma especially when consumed hot. He brought it to his lips savoring a sip of its pleasant flavor as he began to read . . .

\*\*\*\*\*\*\*\*\*\*\*\*\*\*\*\*\*\*\*\*\*\*\*\*\*\*\*\*\*\*\*\*\*\*\*\*\*\*\*\*\*\*\*\*\*\*\*\*\*\*\*\*\*\*\*\*\*\*\*\*\*\*\*\*\*\*\*\*\*\*\*\*\*\*\*\*\*\*\*\*

## United Federation of Worlds, High Council
## Report on:
## United Federation Vessel INFERON
## Coordinated date: 110414

\*\*\*\*\*\*\*\*\*\*\*\*\*\*\*\*\*\*\*\*\*\*\*\*\*\*\*\*\*\*\*\*\*\*\*\*\*\*\*\*\*\*\*\*\*\*\*\*\*\*\*\*\*\*\*\*\*\*\*\*\*\*\*\*\*\*\*\*\*\*\*\*\*\*\*\*\*\*\*\*

Subject:

Reply to requested information regarding Inferon class federation vessels to prospective member planetary system Anasec.

Specific to your request, non-classified general answers to questions regarding federation "Iclass" vessels are provided. Although all three vessels, (Westix, Sagin, and Inferon) are similar in design, function, and capability, this correspondence is specific to the newest and most advanced;

United Federation Vessel INFERON.

The data contained herein is compartmentalized to the following;

Why was it built?
Who designed and built it?
What is its crew contingent?
What is its mission?
What are its capabilities?
Summary

## Why was it built?

The United Federation of Worlds is an organization consisting of more than 5500 individual participant systems and myriads of outposts and settlements, most of which coexist peacefully with one another. These worlds reside within a roughly elliptical volume within the habitable zone centered approximately 50,000 light years from the galactic nucleus. Its own autonomous government governs each individual system. The United

Federation of Worlds provides for the common defense of all systems from outside "alien" invasion, establishes and enforces mutually agreed civil rights, resolves planetary disputes, and negotiates trade agreement policies. The defensive component consists of significant fleets of interstellar vessels and standing armies capable of controlling entire planetary systems.

Deployment of fleet and logistical support resources has been historically slow by comparison to the speed of conflict. Therefore, a first line defense capability became necessary. Three vessels were designed and built for this purpose. These vessels are equipped with advanced capabilities that are intended to be first on scene and formidable enough to slow down even the most well armed and determined aggressor. They function in conjunction with federal fleet resources and report directly to the UFW Central Command Complex located at the world Urianaz.

## Who designed and built it?

The UFV Inferon was designed by some of the most brilliant minds from more than five hundred of the most advanced worlds of the federation. It is therefore a collective product of the United Federation of Worlds itself. Every was detail painstakingly developed by the most advanced technology available. The computer system was built first and would become the central component. This "self-aware" cybernetic intelligent computer could reason, therefore it could also participate in design and construction. Significantly advanced sub system capabilities were designed and incorporated under its guidance. Many thousands of scientists, engineers, technicians, and multitudes of specialized androids participated in the construction of these vessels.

## What is its crew contingent?

Despite its size and capability, the crew consists of seventy living beings and the cybernetic computer system. Since the entire 3.2 billion bases and 35,000 associated genes of the easily manipulated human genome were mapped centuries before, the human species was chosen to be the model for this vessel. Adjustments to the appropriate A-T-G and C base pairs were performed to remove all possible genetic diseases and abnormalities.

Adjustments were also made to enhance physical and mental capabilities necessary for the lifetime task of each individual.

Education and training for each unique crew began shortly after birth and continued to the point of "insertion" into the machines where they will spend the rest of their natural lives. A lifetime for these individuals is based on statistical probability with a standard deviation centered at approximately 700 earth years. The "retirement" of the crew will necessitate decommission and dismantle of the vessel if newer technology warrants or replacement of the crew with a new one if it does not.

## What is its mission?

### Defense:

The primary mission objective is to defend United Federation of Worlds members from aggression, internal or external. It is a device intended to provide an overwhelmingly powerful first line defense in response to acts of aggression in advance of federal fleet forces.

### Mediation:

Providing the platform for mediation between systems in conflict the crew and computer system can be utilized as an ambassador of peace whose purpose is to avoid or put an end to destructive, hostile actions.

### Science:

Its physical capabilities in conjunction with state of the art technology provide the platform by which new discoveries can be studied from a vantage point closer and in finer detail than many of the most advanced science vessels. Data from these discoveries is freely distributed and shared among all participating member systems within the federation.

# What are its capabilities?

## Propulsion:

The UFV Inferon utilizes both NS and ZS propulsion systems.

## Normal space propulsion (NS engines):

NS engines operate in three dimensional "3dim" space and propel the vessel to within .995 light speed. Acceleration in 3dim space exceeds 160,000 feet per second per second (approx 5000 earth g's). 90-degree course changes at full NS speed is accomplished in less than 2 seconds per turn.

## Hyperdrive (ZS engines):

ZS engines operate in zero dimensional "Zdim" space and commonly produce warped space hyperjumps of 5,000 light year distances with longer jump capabilities if needed.

## Defensive armament:

The exterior hull is formed as a single crystal polydiametic solid metallic lattice. There are no exterior doors, ports, or other access to the interior. All transfer of matter in or out of these vessels is via matter-energy transporters. The general shape and dimension is approximately 7 miles long x 3 miles wide x 1 mile.

In addition to the physical hull, a classified number of force field shields surround the entire vessel. These shields are independently phased to confuse or block any incoming projectile, plasma, or energy weapon. The shields also function as energy absorbing sinks. Energy absorbed during an attack can be redirected into its own systems.

## Offensive armament:

Weapon systems are incorporated for a wide variety of applications:

## Close order, small targets:

Pulsed laser, and focused plasma can be targeted against numerous targets simultaneously.

Simultaneous target numbers and individual pulsed laser and plasma energies are classified.

Targeting is accurate to 99.95%.

## Large targets, hardened vessels, and planetary bases:

High-energy plasma and "knife energy" weapons can be utilized to vaporize large targets or to cut them into smaller pieces. The knife energy beam has an adjustable width and involves matter disruption energies.

## Planetary scale or very large military armadas:

Antimatter launch systems are available for deployment against very large targets or military installations. These systems produce antimatter with minimum quantities under an ounce and maximum quantities large enough to produce a planetary destabilization event. The antimatter core is protected by strong deflection fields and can be steered during transit.

# Information and communication systems:

## Internal:

The cybernetic intelligent computer system is the primary information-processing device. It is a massive multi level neural net processor designed around molecular polyemetic crystal lattice core technology. It is capable of high order reasoning, emotion emulation, and internal-external multi task functions. It is a sentient self-aware, synthetic life form, and a member of the crew. It is capable of interaction on a mental "pseudo telepathic" level utilizing beta wave modulators. Hence the acronym CIMDI; Cybernetic Intelligent Mental Direct Interconnect. The specific technology remains classified.

Anything CIMDI sees or senses with its myriad of sensors can be mentally conveyed into the mind of the captain and leading members of the crew. Those crewmembers can also mentally convey information and instructions to the CIMDI system.

## External:

The UFV Inferon utilizes both 3com and Zcom communication systems.

## Local:

Three-dimensional communications "3com" is utilized in close proximity.

## Interstellar:

Zero dimensional communications "Zcom" is utilized for interstellar communication.

## Person to person:

External personal communications are conducted via the Hypercybergenic form generator system (HCG for short). This system is similar to an old style transporter except that it creates a replica of the user at a remote location. Through the CIMDI system, the user "projects" him/her self mentally into the HCG form and experience all five senses as if physically present. Anything the HCG form experiences the user experiences (with the exception of pain or death). This feature is of particular use during negotiations. The CIMDI system automatically translates language allowing the user to communicate in his/her native language. The HCG form communicates in the indigenous language.

## Misc communications:

The CIMDI system has the ability to scan the computer system on an aggressor vessel regardless of its protection systems. Information obtained in this way is used first to alleviate hostility, second to disable, shut down, or take control of the aggressor, and lastly to determine weakness.

Constant communication is maintained between all three "Iclass" vessels and the master system located at the central command complex on Urianaz via Zcom. Since the master system and all CIMDI systems are in perpetual contact, no decision of any importance is made on an independent level.

**Maintenance and upgrades:**

The General Systems Specialists direct maintenance functions that can't be handled by the CIMDI system directly. Via specialized function androids, the Inferon can repair or "heal" itself. Replacement components are automatically upgraded to the latest design advancement.

# Misc. systems and functions:

**Navigation systems:**

These systems contain a complete database of every known celestial body. Updated on a real time basis to account for known velocity and gravitational interaction, navigation to a specific point in close proximity to moving celestial bodies is extremely accurate.

**Science platform:**

A wide variety of advanced observation, measuring, and testing systems analyze all forms of physical phenomena as well as coordinate, organize, and disseminate scientific observations and data.

# Summary:

The United Federation Vessel INFERON is one of three most powerful and versatile devices within the federation. Only the fastest ships exceed its speed and maneuverability. Its CIMDI controlled armament is unmatched. Its defensive hull and associated shielding make it nearly impenetrable.

The intent of these is to protect United Federation of Worlds member systems from all aggressors. To date this strategy has been an effective tool for deterrence. In most cases, the arrival of one of these vessels has been sufficient to alleviate hostility. In the rare case where aggression was attempted the power of one or more of these vessels was brought to bear and efficiently ended the conflict.

Further questions can be directed through appropriate channels to the United Federation of Worlds, Strategic Sciences Command, Urianaz.

End of Message.

# Ch 2

## Anasec

*"Fishing is much more than fish. It is the great occasion when we may return to the fine simplicity of our forefathers."*
*Herbert Hoover*

Commander Iss took a slow breath and swallowed the last sip of derf in his cup. *"Impressive and unsettling at the same time,"* he thought as he mulled over the transmission. Sub-Commander Ciris approached just as he finished reading. She was dressed impeccably in the uniform of the day. He liked that in his crew . . . To see them show pride in the uniform they wore. He believed showing attention to detail regarding the uniform also revealed something important about the wearer's attitude. Sub-Commander Ciris was especially attentive to that detail. Every crease was straight and every medal exactly aligned.

"Reading the report I see. What do you think Commander?"

"Concerned might be a good word," he replied pointing to the display as he spoke.

"I've heard rumors and seen unofficial reports like many others but this describes something that exceeds even the exaggerated claims."

He looked straight at Sub-C Ciris, "If these things are as capable as this report describes they can be a powerful ally to be sure. But they can also be a dreadful adversary."

She thought for a moment, "Yes sir you might be right. No insult intended but they do make ours seem outdated."

"Outdated and probably outgunned," Commander Iss replied knitting his forehead in a concerned look.

Ciris started, "Yes but . . ."

"And another thing, "he said raising two fingers to silence her sentence. "Our vessel is only marginally bigger than this 'Iclass' vessel yet its crew is only seventy! Our crew compliment exceeds twenty thousand."

"That is curious," she admitted.

"Yes." Commander Iss said narrowing his eyes. "That means almost everything on the ship they describe is automated. Putting that much power under the control of a computer is dangerous in my opinion."

Sub-C Ciris thought for a moment, "Perhaps their technology has advanced far enough that their computers are trustworthy to the point of infallibility, sir."

Commander Iss smiled, "Now that's optimism. I hope you're right."

"I hope so too," Sub-C Ciris replied relaxing a bit. "They're supposed to be the good guys."

"That's what they say," Commander Iss added. "But if that's wrong and they ever do go rouge we'll have a nasty battle on our hands."

"Well sir I hardly think they'll do that. After all, they've apparently been around for almost three hundred years. Their record is flawless. Aside from that, they're all equipped with fail safe and remote destruct systems. If one of them ever did go rouge the UFW Central Command would eliminate it." Sub-C Ciris stopped to take a breath then continued in a more subdued tone.

Leaning toward her commander as if to tell a secret she continued, "Besides they're just the tip of the spear sir. As a member of the federation we'll be part of the blade behind it."

Commander Iss thought for a moment focusing his gaze to the stars outside again, "That's a nice way to put it. But like I just said, power like that makes me uneasy."

Sub-C Ciris smiled, "Perhaps you'll feel differently when you see one and meet its captain, sir."

Commander Iss looked back at her questioningly, "Oh. When will that be?"

Straightening a bit, "Soon sir, we've just received orders to return home to Anasec. The votes have been counted and it's now official. Anasec is to join the United Federation of Worlds."

Commander Iss didn't reply as he returned his gaze to the stars outside.

She waited for a moment, "We're assigned to be the flagship escort for the federation entourage at Anasec . . . It will include the UFV Inferon sir."

Still looking at the stars outside Commander Iss spoke with a hint of quiet concern in his voice, "The vessel described in the transmission?"

"The same sir," Sub-C Ciris replied. "The Paquet and about half a dozen others are to be part of the welcoming escort at Anasec next month."

"Hmm, that soon huh?" Commander Iss questioned.

"Yes sir. The orders arrived while you were reading. That's what I was waiting to tell you."

"Okay then," Commander Iss replied. "We'll proceed to Anasec and greet this Federation vessel."

"Since we're going to join the UFW it might help to see the vessel they described in this message anyway."

During the following weeks, Commander Iss engaged in conference meetings with the other commanders who would participate with the welcoming escort. They discussed various formations, weapon readiness, and formal protocol. Together they formed a plan that would provide an honorable welcome to the federation vessel when it arrived over Anasec. The last few days passed quickly as they traveled to Anasec and made final preparations for the visit.

Bix sat in his boat a mile or so off shore on the East Sea fishing with his son Nuw. Unlike most Anasecians, Bix enjoyed the "connection" as he often called using a boat that floated on the water rather than a hovercraft that remained just above it. Hovercraft *just didn't feel right* to him. The boat was an elegant little vessel with a battery powered propeller propulsion system.

"Please pass the bait box son," he asked.

"Here dad," Nuw replied passing the box.

It was a nice day with the sun shining through breaks between puffy white clouds in the otherwise blue sky overhead. A light breeze stirred up small waves atop the gently rolling swells arriving from far out at sea.

"*A wonderful day to spend with a child fishing*," Bix thought to himself as he baited the hook and cast his line into the water.

Nuw asked, "There aren't any Onxfish around here are there?"

"I don't think so," he replied glancing down at the function lights on the protective shield generator under the seat.

His thoughts drifted to them for a moment.

Onxfish where widely distributed in the oceans and seas of Anasec. Maturing in thirty years or so, Onxfish grew to as much as forty feet in length, twice that of his boat. With mouths equipped with sharp eight-inch long teeth, they were the apex predators of the sea and the terror of the deep. They were notorious for attacking and eating just about anything that moved. He'd only seen one once when he was younger. On that occasion, it approached his boat and attempted to attack. Fortunately, the protective shield generator automatically deployed and prevented him and his boat from becoming lunch. It protected him from sudden inclement weather a couple of times too.

"Besides, our little box under the seat here will protect us if one of them ever does come around," he reassured with a smile.

Not very satisfied with his dad's words Nuw returned to fiddling with his own fishing gear.

"Would like to see one though," Nuw said in a low tone over his shoulder.

"Uh, you might think so son but trust me, you wouldn't," Bix explained patiently. "Even with the protective shield a close up look at all three jaws of an Onxfish crashing down on it is a pretty scary experience."

Nuw was about to say something else when the com link chimed with its pleasantly female tone, "Incoming call from Wiml."

"Accept call."

"Hey Bix, how are you today my friend?" came a familiar voice over the com.

"Not bad," he replied humoring his friend. "What's on your mind? And it better be good because Nuw and I are busy trying to catch dinner," he added with a snicker.

"Not out in that little boat again are you?" Wiml replied ignoring the question for a moment.

Bix answered his friend as he looked out over the water, "Oh yea. There's nothing like the sound of the waves lapping against the side of the boat. Besides, anyone can go out in a hovercraft. The old-fashioned way is better. It makes me feel more connected."

"Whatever suits you my friend, just watch for the big ones," Wiml said chuckling.

Nuw's eyes widened just a bit overhearing the conversation.

Bix paused for a moment, "You didn't call to talk about fishing and boats. What's on your mind, Wiml?"

"Just thought you should know we'll be getting together next week at Ina."

"I thought so," Bix replied. "The final votes were counted and verified weeks ago. I figured that an acceptance meeting was coming soon. Do you have the date?"

"Yep. We will be getting together next week on the third day of the moon. Check your commail when you get home for the specifics. Oh, and I already have a room reserved for you and Minsi. You owe me one," Wiml teased.

"Will do. What would I do without a friend like you? See you in a week," Bix replied. "End call."

Nuw, forgetting about "big ones" turned to his dad excitedly, "Can mom and I go with you?"

"Certainly. This is a big deal. I want you and your mom to be there. So unless she's got obligations she can't get out of we'll all go to Ina together."

"Really nice nice!" Nuw said enthusiastically. He was too young to understand the significance of the meeting his dad was planning to attend. He simply enjoyed the adventure of going to the big city.

That evening Bix spoke about the upcoming trip with his wife Minsi as they dined on the fish him and his son caught that day.

"Oh I would really enjoy going to Ina with you," she replied. "I'll arrange to take time off at the pharmacy."

"I'm glad you said that my wife. For this occasion I'm glad we can all go there together." he added smiling.

He always enjoyed it when she would go with him on business trips and especially wanted her to accompany him on this one. After all this was an historic occasion and he wanted his family to be part of it. Even though she couldn't be at the meeting proper she and his son would be there at Ina with him. He liked finding opportunities to go out with her anyway.

"Perhaps we can take time to go out on the town while we're there too," he said with a suggestive grin.

"I'll count on that," she replied. "We haven't gone out for a while."

"I know. It's easy to get so tied up in responsibilities that the important things get left out," he lamented.

Taking another bite of the fresh catch of the day she complimented them, "This fish is really good."

Nuw sat up proudly in his chair, "I caught that one mom. It was a real fighter too!" he added.

"I'll bet it was," she replied smiling as her gaze returned to her husband.

He just smiled back enjoying his dinner and the company of his wife sitting across from him.

She was a very attractive Anasecian female. Tall, delicate, large dark round eyes, and the most beautiful blue-green skin he had ever seen. The following week they traveled to Ina where they checked into the motel, did a little shopping, dined with Wiml and other friends, and settled in. The next day would be an important day.

# CH 3

## MEMBERSHIP

*"For time and the world do not stand still. Change is the
law of life. And those who look only to the past or the present
are certain to miss the future."*
*John F. Kennedy*

Bix and Wiml walked down the corridor of the east wing of the
complex on their way to the central meeting area. The atriplex as it was
called was a seven sided meeting rotunda in the center of a sprawling
government complex. The seating and desk space to accommodate almost
a thousand dignitaries and representatives was arranged to focus upon the
central podium where heads of state would often speak. Windows high up
on the dome allowed natural light in. Framed upon its sides were pictures
depicting the history of their world, prominent heads of state, landmark
historic events, and the joining of all governments into a combined union
several hundred years before.

The whole complex was busy with people going back and forth, as they
got ready for the historic meeting. Bix and his colleague Wiml represented
population zones that shared a border along the East Sea. They'd grown
up together, attended the same schools, and were good friends for most
of their lives.

"I've been waiting for this for a long time," Bix commented as they
walked along.

"Me too. I understand a number of the UFW leadership will address
the council today."

"That's my understanding," Wiml replied. "I hear one of those ships, the vessel Inferon will be somewhere overhead as well. But during the daylight we probably won't see it."

"No, probably not. But the escorts up there will provide a video feed so we'll be able to see it that way."

"That'll be interesting," Wiml commented.

"Yes it will," agreed Bix. "I understand that not many people actually get to see one of them."

"True." Wiml replied, "But I've heard a rumor that the high counsel authorized the federation vessel to perform some kind of special inspection maneuver that may allow us to see it."

Bix thought for a moment, "The phrase 'special presentation' in the agenda is vague. No one seems to know the details. But if we were to be able to see their vessel that would truly be interesting."

"Perhaps that's why the rumor originated. And yes, you're right, that would be." commented Wiml.

They entered the central meeting atriplex and found their seats. As he got comfortable, Bix reached down into his attaché for a small pouch and a cup. "Would you like some?"

"Maybe later, but thanks for the offer." Wiml replied thumbing through his papers.

He wanted to review his notes during the half hour or so before the meeting. Bix tore the pouch at the indicated corner and poured its contents into the cup. Immediately hot as it contacted the air his cup was soon filled with a favorite beverage, the tart, spicy elixir called hot Ansbria cider.

Commander Iss ordered his ship moved into the prescribed position in orbit. The central government city of Ina would come up over the horizon on the daylight side in about twenty minutes.

He relaxed for a moment letting his mind drift to thoughts about Ina. It was a beautiful city situated on the west shore of Lake Ina. Located several hundred miles inland from the Askeen Ocean at a temperate latitude it was a tropical city with a moderate climate. It was also the seat of the unified government on his world, and had a reported population of just over twelve million. He remembered attending the academy there, vacationing in the mountains to the north, and courting females in its social places. It had been a long time since the last time he'd been there.

Today wouldn't change that. It was business and the closest he'd get to the place this time would be a couple hundred miles above.

"Sensor readings?"

"None sir," replied Tactical Officer Hadu. "The only vessels are ours sir."

"*Hmm,*" thought Iss. "*Where was this mysterious ship?*"

They continued scanning the sky for an incoming vessel but other than scheduled commercial vessels and freighters arriving or leaving from other cities in this hemisphere the UFW ship they were watching for wasn't there. A couple more minutes passed before all the scanners, cameras, and other detection equipment alerted them to the presents of a large vessel approaching from behind.

"Tactical. There it is, directly astern sir. Twenty degrees above!"

"Screens, visual please," Commander Iss requested calmly.

The aft video feed flooded the viewer screen. There it was. The first any of them had seen of one of those federation vessels. They were told it would be the UFV Inferon but there were no markings to confirm that upon its hull. "*It wasn't quite as big as his ship,*" thought Commander Iss. As it approached, the command crew of his ship all seemed to notice the same remarkable details.

The approaching vessel was shaped roughly like a smoothly contoured wedge. From the nearly pointed bow the elegant lines of vessel widened out and thickened toward the aft end to about one third the total width of the vessel. To each side were slightly down sloped tapered sections that terminated in what appeared to be defection panels of some kind. On the top near the aft end, the keel line sloped up smoothly into a raised section assumed to house the command bridge. No hatches or lights were visible to indicate accesses or windows to the interior. In fact, its entire surface was very smooth, and glowed with a very faint blue-gray luminance. It had no antenna arrays, sensor portals, or weapons visible upon its surface. It did have blue luminous stripes visible on the sloping surfaces to the left and right of both the upper and lower keel lines that ran the length of the vessel. Similar luminous blue lines ran along the outer edges and along the aft facing edges.

"It's so clean," commented Sub Commander Ciris in a hushed voice.

"There aren't any laser cannons mounted on the outside of that thing," said someone else.

"I wonder what purpose the blue lines serve?" questioned Science Leader Kymm.

"And where are its com antennas, sensor portals, or gun mountings"?

With his mind set on the more important issues Commander Iss asked, "Why we didn't see it until it was right on our six like that?"

"Must have an advance cloaking shield of some kind," replied Science Leader Kymm. "There was no sensor data until it reveled itself sir."

Tactical Officer Hadu added, "It doesn't look anything like I thought it would from the report. I thought it would bristle with weaponry and sensors. But none are visible."

Commander Iss concurred, "Yes, it conceals its true capability behind an elegant appearance and smooth lines. That sort of thing has always made me nervous."

A moment later he added, "Be prepared for stationary hover."

The navigation officer looked at him with puzzlement, "Hover!"

"You heard me." Commander Iss answered. "We've been notified to plan on a stationary hover over Ina. Notify all escort ships."

"Sorry sir," the Navigation officers stated, "We haven't done that maneuver in quite a while, that's all."

"Understood." Commander Iss replied. He wasn't particularly concerned with the energy demands of a hover maneuver.

They'd been directly behind and above the group of Anasecian vessels for some time. Captain Marc chose to keep the Inferon concealed until they could assess them. Five vessels were arranged in a "V" shaped formation. The command vessel Paquet was positioned inside the "V" to the left. An obvious space was provided to the right of it within their formation.

Captain Marc thought about their participation in the acceptance of another world into the federation. It pleased him. It was far better than being engaged in a military conflict that cost lives. Even though Captain Marc and the rest of the crew were charged with defending the federation, the use of force was something he preferred to avoid. That was probably the reason why so many federation leaders thought of him as such an excellent negotiator. The truth was that he'd negotiate with every bit of his knowledge and skill to avoid a senseless confrontation.

CIMDI provided Tactical Specialist Siven and Captain Marc a complete mentally inserted tactical assessment. Although the vessels ahead had set their weapons to standby along the outer side of the "V" formation the inner ones were all in stand down mode. No threat was detected. Hidden deep within the core processor a thousand simulated scenarios played out and each one was secretly assessed. If in the remotest chance something undesirable did occur CIMDI would already have a plan in place to deal with it.

Sitting in his chair behind and slightly above several of his command crew, Captain Marc had a full view. A large seamless view screen around the smooth curve of the command bridge provided an excellent 270 deg view. The bridge was constructed somewhat like that of a theater balcony in the sense that the view screen extended both above and below the command deck as well as to the sides allowing for a view that appeared as if the command bridge were floating in space. The view could be presented as a tactical display or as a representation of infrared, ultraviolet, gravity wave, or a composite display of several at once. Presently his view was of the Anasecian vessels set against the backdrop of the planet below. Their shiny hulls reflected the light from the sun as they approached the daylight side. Beyond them, the brightly colored planet hung in stark contrast against the backdrop of the star filled blackness of space. Oceans and continents could be seen between clouds that gleamed in the light as they all passed across the terminator from the night side to the dayside. Captain Marc could see a complete three-dimensional view of everything around them provided by the ingenious technology of the mental direct interconnect of the CIMDI system if he chose. Presently he looked around the command bridge with his own eyes . . .

"Are we ready for contact Tactical Specialist Siven?"

"Yes sir. All vessel scans normal. Threat assessment minimal."

"Very well then. Secure the concealment field."

"Yes sir. Securing the concealment field," answered Tactical Specialist Siven. "We are now visible."

"Nav Specialist Inia . . . Position us to the right of the command vessel within their "V" formation. Match position and velocity."

"Moving now," she answered.

The huge ship began to move into position with the welcome escort from Anasec.

Captain Marc instructed Com Specialist Jiin to open a communications channel to their vessels. He began to speak.

A voice came over the Anasecian vessel communications links, "We are Inferon. Request visitation upon your world to confer as arranged. Do you allow?"

Commander Iss was the leader of the welcoming vessels and thus answered, "Permission granted. Welcome to Anasec."

He was being politically polite, and following orders. Commander Iss quietly thought to himself, "*do you allow . . . Hmmm.*"

The UFV Inferon slid silently into position to the right of the command vessel Paquet within the formation. It looked defenseless next to an entourage of military vessels armed to the teeth with laser and plasma cannons, sensor arrays, and other armament. To the seasoned military mind of Commander Iss its smooth lines and apparent vulnerability were an illusion. Outwardly, he displayed an air of confidence and control to his crew. Inwardly he couldn't escape the uncomfortable feeling that if it chose to do so, what he saw out there could probably dispatch every one of them.

As they approached two hundred miles above Ina, the Inferon began to slow. The escort ships matched speed and slowed as well. Coming to a stop they all became motionless directly over the city far below. Without the centrifugal balance of orbital velocity, a large amount of energy was required to hold a fifteen billion ton ship like the Paquet in a stationary hover, but it was ordered and accomplished. All the ships hovered motionless high above Ina. Commander Iss knew from his classified report what was to happen next. He'd argued unsuccessfully against it. As the Inferon began to descend downward Captain Marc spoke over the Anasecian com channel, "We will now present the UFV Inferon to the people of Anasec for their inspection." That was something none of the escort vessels could do! They were purely creatures of space. Commander Iss and his crew could only watch as the huge vessel entered the atmosphere below.

Commander Iss tensed, "*If it became necessary to do so, how could we protect our world from this without significant loss of life?*" He tried to comfort himself by remembering Sub Commander Ciris's words last month . . . "*They're supposed to be the good guys.*" and "*After all they've apparently been around for almost three hundred years. Their record is flawless.*" Far below a gossamer layer of high altitude cirrus clouds parted as the vessel passed through them on its way down to Ina. Commander Iss sat quietly in his command chair watching. Everyone around him was too busy doing their jobs to notice their commanders fingers dug deep into the armrest cushions of his seat.

Bix took a sip of his cider before setting the cup on the desk space to his side. Almost unnoticed at first the liquid in his cup began to tremble.

Wiml noticed it first, "What's with that?"

"What's with what?" Bix replied.

"That." Wiml said, pointing to the cup on his desk.

Small concentric ripples caused by a vibration in the desk appeared in the liquid.

Soon they felt it in their seats and on the floor below their feet. A murmur from the crowd made it clear they were not the only ones to notice. Everything was vibrating with a quiet low frequency tremor. The video screens answered the question. The huge ship was carefully settling into a hover a mile above and just to their east putting most of it out over the waters of Lake Ina. A light breeze kicked up as the air pushed out from between it and the ground. Everything for miles became shaded from the sun by its immense shadow. The view of such a large object positioned motionless so close to the surface was almost surrealistic. Nobody on Anasec had ever seen anything like that before! People everywhere stopped what they were doing to gaze up at the spectacle overhead. Some remained motionless as if frozen in their tracks, staring skyward. Many others became fearful and headed for cover. Near the center under the vessel where it was the deepest shadow, the hull glowed with a faint metallic blue pulsating light that made it look almost alive.

At the motel Minsi and her son Nuw were watching the proceedings at the atriplex on the view screen. A second screen provided a view of the strange vessel descending toward Ina as seen from the escort vessels high above. A low rumble began as the bright sunlight coming through the balcony windows darkened in shadow. Nuw's hearts were beating faster but curiosity got the best of him. He moved hesitantly to the balcony door and looked out.

"Mom, mom!" he said excitedly as he quickly backed away from the door.

Reaching her, he quickly put his arms around her waist. Wide-eyed and suddenly afraid she couldn't tell if it was Nuw trembling or the low rumble apparent in everything else.

"It's okay son," she replied calmly. "It must be one of those protector ships your dad told us about on the way here."

"I'm scared mom," he admitted. "I don't like this."

"I know, I know. But it won't hurt you," she said attempting to reassure him even though her own hearts were beating faster too. "Let's go take a look together okay?"

"No mom no! I don't want to," Nuw pleaded.

"It'll be alright," she persisted in her attempt to reassure him. "Look out there. See, it goes way out over Lake Ina." she said pointing to the balcony door and the view out toward the lake.

He began to relax slightly as she continued to sooth his fear with her calm voice.

Minsi moved toward the door and out onto the motel balcony where they could get a better view. Nuw maintained his tight grip as he followed her to the door.

"Wow!" she said in amazement looking up at the spectacle above. She'd never seen anything so big so close to the ground before.

The gleaming metallic blue underside of the huge ship hung motionless above them. Even though she was secretly frightened herself, she couldn't help but notice its smooth lines. She had to admit, even thought its size scared her it didn't look like the holograms of military or science vessels she'd seen before. It was somehow . . . "Pretty."

Nuw who'd kept his eyes closed stole a glance from under his moms arm. He didn't notice that many other people standing on the street below were looking up with the same anxiety and amazement.

Upon the central podium, several figures materialized.

Leaning over Bix whispered to Wiml, "Is that what a 'human' looks like?"

"I guess so," Wiml answered. "Five fingered creatures with dirt colored skin."

Compared to Anasecians, humans were a bit shorter and thicker. They also had two more fingers and ears that protruded from the sides of their heads rather than near the top like Anasecians did. Most of the members of the meeting had never seen a human form before.

"From the report I didn't think anyone from the crew ever left their ship," commented Bix in a whisper.

"They sure look real don't they, but they're not. Especially the Captain, the one dressed in all black. He's a temporary duplicate of some kind," Wiml replied quietly.

Bix thought for a moment as he studied them then whispered back, "How can that be? He looks real to me. He's certainly no hologram."

Wiml pointed to a paragraph in his notes, "No. The Captain of the Inferon never leaves the ship. None of its crew ever does. What we see is a copy the computer system on the ship somehow connects to the real

Captain, uh, Marc I believe is his name, who is probably sitting on its bridge right now."

The one dressed in black stepped forward. He was an average size human male who appeared to be in his late thirties, maybe early forties. He had a medium build, dressed impeccably in black trousers and a seamless shirt. His exposed features appeared hairless with a medium tanned complexion.

He spoke; "I am Marc, Captain of the United Federation Vessel Inferon. On behalf of myself, the crew, and the United Federation of Worlds council, thank you for the invitation to Anasec and the beautiful city of Ina. The United Federation Vessel Inferon awaits your inspection. You may dispatch vessels to investigate but approach no closer than five hundred feet to avoid interference with protective shielding. May I present the leaders of the United Federation of Worlds Core Council?" Stepping to one side, he proceeded to introduce each of the Federation High Council members who appeared with him. Bix listened with all the others as formalities, greetings, and speeches were delivered. All the while, the quiet rumble continued in everything around him. He understood just as everyone else did. It was the unmistakable whisper of very great power.

From the power plant management center the propulsion engineer called over the intercom, "Commander Iss, we can't maintain stationary status for more than a couple hours at a time. The engines are straining to maintain position against the gravity."

"Understood."

He instructed the com officer to send instructions to move half the escort back to orbit velocity and leave the other half here.

Commander Iss and two others would move first, giving the engines a break from the strain. When they'd complete an orbit and come back around they'd stop and let the rest of the escort do the same. In this way, there would always be an escort overhead and no vessel would suffer damage from overstrained propulsion systems. Down near the surface the UFV Inferon experienced no such issue. Remaining motionless during the entire meeting process the mind of the Inferon, CIMDI barely noticed.

# CH4

## QUEEN AREAN

*"You must either conquer and rule or serve and lose, suffer or triumph, be the anvil or the hammer."*
*Johann Wolfgang von Goethe*

The signing of the agreement was completed with all the required signatures, and was followed with a customary celebration party. Captain Marc invited several of his command crew to the surface in their HCG forms to join the celebration. As they appeared, he introduced each one. Later in the afternoon, Captain Marc found himself engaged in conversation with several dignitaries of the Ansecian council.

"So, what is it like to be the captain of the Inferon?" one of them asked.

"It is all that I know," Captain Marc replied. "So my frame of reference is somewhat limited. I will say that it's an honor to serve the federation and to serve you," he added.

"Have you ever had an incident where force was used when it didn't need to be?" asked another.

"Every time," Captain Marc replied. "If force is applied it's because diplomacy failed in some way or another."

"So you've never had to defend the federation against a completely unwilling enemy?"

"I can't say that. There was the incident at Romual about fifty years ago."

"What happened there?" one of the dignitaries asked with a curious look on her face.

"An armada of Reasnolics attacked the federation world of Romual with no provocation or warning. We attempted to negotiate but they simply refused to answer our offer." Pointing in the direction of Weapons Specialist Seale he continued, "Weapons Specialist Seale whose standing over there chatting with that group used an antimatter pulse against a nearby dead moon as a demonstration. A shot over the bow as it were. Even that didn't work. So we did what we had to do to protect our member world."

"My, my," said someone else in the group. "I'll bet that was impressive."

"Yes it was," replied Captain Marc, "but ineffective. The situation forced the Inferon to eliminate more than half their fleet before they capitulated. Many died for no gain."

"How did that make you feel?"

"Sad." Captain Marc answered. "Force is and must always be the last resort."

Changing the subject another dignitary asked Captain Marc what the HCG form system is like and how he felt about the intrusion of the CIMDI system into his mind.

Captain Marc explained;

"The HCG form allows us to leave the Inferon without risking disease or injury. In fact it's the only way we're able to interact on a personal level outside the vessel. In addition, with the exception of minor details, experiencing the environment through an HCG form is much like experiencing it through my own body. The added benefit of its ability to translate language makes communication delightful. Being able to communicate directly with CIMDI is a powerful tool too. I can see things through it that unaided biological eyes cannot see. Information from it, and commands to it are much faster."

Across the room, Nav Specialist Inia was conferring with a small group of Anasecian astro-scientists.

"How complex is the navigation database on your ship?" one asked.

Nav Specialist Inia smiled, "The database is complete to the point that it accounts for the gravitational interaction of all objects as small as the moons or Urianaz or the moon of earth within and near federation space. Outside that volume all stellar sized objects within this half of our galaxy are also mapped."

"That's amazing! To apply second and third order linear differential mathematics to that many elements at once must require monumental computational resources," the scientist remarked.

"Yes," Nav Specialist Inia replied;

"It does. However, the system simplifies the process by creating a three dimensional gas matrix simulation. Each celestial body is assigned a number relative to its mass, a vector to describe its movement, and its position relative to all others in the galactic plane. The gas in the simulation draws toward the mass of a planet or star at a rate proportional to its mass index number, which creates differences in gas density. Celestial bodies are then carried in the current created by the density differences. An asteroid for example, moves toward the lower gas density produced by a large object such as a planet. The simulation emulates gravitons that produce gravitational interaction so well that we can exit Zdim space very close to the last known position of a planet without concern for colliding with it."

One of the other scientists asked Nav Specialist Inia if it were possible to obtain a copy of the algorithm used to create the star map.

She replied, "Now that you're part of the United Federation of Worlds you are entitled to information such as this. Contact the UFW Strategic Sciences Center at Urianaz and they will prepare a copy of the program for you. You will need a level five multi-layered neural net processor and about fifty terabytes of combined data storage capacity to run it. The algorithm aboard the Inferon is not available due to additional classified details."

"I understand, and thank you. This will be a stimulating experience for all of us I'm sure."

"You're very welcome," said Nav Specialist Inia with a smile. She was about to continue the conversation when she was interrupted by a message from CIMDI . . .

The Captain Marc HCG form suddenly stopped talking with a group of Anasecian dignitaries. "Pardon me for just a moment." Standing motionless for a moment, he appeared as if pondering a sudden thought, and then turned to the people he'd been talking with.

"I apologize," he said, "An emergency calls us away. We must depart presently. Please forgive our apparent rudeness."

One of the dignitaries asked, "What emergency calls you away?"

"An armada of warships has approached and attacked the Queen Arean system. We must depart immediately to render support." Moments later, he and the rest of the crew who were visiting with him dematerialized and were gone.

One of the UFW dignitaries spoke up to the rest of the people present. "We apologize for the sudden departure. Inferon has been called away to address a disturbance in the Queen Arean system. But we will remain to continue the celebration of our new alliance together."

The low rumble intensified slightly as the huge ship began to rise. Moving very slowly at first to avoid potentially damaging wind caused by the movement of such a large vessel it lifted away and began to pitch bow up. It was a spectacular sight to those on the ground as it aligned itself vertically and began moving slowly away from them into the sky. Its faceted aft sections glowed bright blue two miles or more above them. Its forward section and bow were almost out of sight many miles beyond as it lifted away, accelerating as distance and thinning air allowed. Passing through the thinnest upper atmosphere, it began to accelerate rapidly.

Aboard the Paquet, Commander Iss and the rest of the crew watched it leave a flickering luminous trail of ionized air in its wake as it left the rarefied upper atmosphere behind. Commander Iss breathed a sigh of relief. Before he could relax the com channel opened again. "Commander Iss, should you desire, the coordinates are ($r$ 336.23, $\theta$ 7.05, $\varphi$ 34.3) from this location. If you choose to follow, observe only, do not engage, and do not interfere." Before he could think much about how the Inferon captain knew his name it accelerated away, vanishing from the view screens and sensor tracking as suddenly as it arrived earlier that day.

"Lead Command Council, Commander Paquet . . . Request permission to follow."

"Standby for reply." About half an hour later, a voice came over the com. "Commander Iss, the primary defense delegation has determined that a first hand observation would be very informative. Therefore, you are authorized to take two escorts and proceed to the coordinates provided. Report back."

Commander Iss acknowledged the order then turned to his navigation officer, "Set the coordinates into the navigation computer and prepare for transit to the location provided." He contacted two of the other ships and ordered them to follow. He also ordered the remaining ships to assume tactical defensive positions around Anasec until their return. As the Paquet and its escort prepared to depart toward the coordinates provided by the captain of the federation vessel the shadow of a dark thought crossed his mind, "*Isn't this a convenient coincidence. Lure the defense command vessels to a destination far away for convenient disposal leaving the home world vulnerable to attack by another of those ships.*" Just as quickly, his logic returned, "*No . . . With the power those things had they wouldn't need such a ruse.*"

"Coordinates loaded and ready sir."

"Let's proceed . . . Engage engines, maximum hyperdrive as soon as we're clear of Anasec gravity field."

Three ships joined in a tactical formation and accelerated toward unfamiliar space more than three thousand light years away.

Having joined the federation centuries before Queen Arean became a desired vacation destination. It was adorned with breathtaking panoramas, exquisite natural beauty, and abundant resources. It had high ice covered peaks within vast forested mountain ranges separated by expansive prairie and grasslands. Its giant meadows were splashed with vibrant carpets of red, violet, yellow, and white flowers. Those who experienced them often described these places with accolades like "legendary," "breathtaking," and "inspiring." Queen Arean also had the distinction of the deepest oceans of any world in the federation. Many visitors enjoyed sightseeing trips to the bottom of the sea where more than twenty miles of water separated them from the surface. There one could witness the spectacular photo luminescence of creatures that lived in the perpetual freezing darkness of the deep.

It's intelligent civilization was comprised of a race of beings who lived and worked in precisely arranged and geometrically organized cities. Buildings within them were commonly constructed using blue or yellow marble facades and stood as high as a half mile above the streets. Interspersed with parks, waterways, and exquisitely manicured green spaces, even the cities held a beauty rarely seen anywhere else in the federation. Eerily similar to the honeycombed networks of earth's bees, Alpha Cette's Cazaba flies, and the Kroana bees of Enif, those who visited Queen Arean often remarked that its cities could almost be thought of as "hives." Across the planet, numerous queens were prepared via special nutrients prior to birth to function as the leaders of their respective zone. All the regional queens, the drones and workers who served them, and all the "common ones" lived in a hierarchical social order leading up to the royal palace and the most respected and revered queen of them all, the planets namesake, Queen Arean herself.

For all its beauty and allure, the Queen Arean world had its problems too. It endured years of harassment from a race of warlike beings from outside the federation. Queen Arean knew little about them because they completely ignored attempts at negotiation and rarely communicated about anything else. Over the years, small groups of them attacked isolated outposts and small settlements with increasing frequency. Responding to the harassment Queen Arean dispatched defensive forces and called upon the UFW for additional support when the attacks became more severe.

In response to her request a contingent of UFW military vessels were stationed there to help protect them from such incidents. Nevertheless, their presents didn't seem to deter the number of incursions by the aggressors.

The great halls that housed the queens had long ago removed themselves from direct exposure to unfiltered information due to its inherently incorrect, contradictory, and sometimes deliberately misinformed nature, but they were not isolated. Each queen had an information gathering and summarizing entourage with whom she trusted implicitly. Large numbers of workers prepared information the queen received from her messengers. It was checked carefully for accuracy and completeness before any messenger approached the great hall to provide it. Any messenger discovered providing misinformation to its queen faced immediate consequences for its actions, and permanent removal from her service. She also communicated directly with the lower queens of her world. It was from these information sources that decisions were made.

Knowing from previous reports that a large armada was approaching her world, Queen Arean summoned her messenger. She wanted to know the latest information regarding the intent and purpose of the intrusion. Moving down the great hall the messenger moved as quickly as its four legs could carry it. With each step, its feet made a clicking sound that echoed back and forth between the great walls. In its hands, it carried a computer display pad with the information it intended to convey. The glass smooth floor on which it moved was adorned with beautifully colored motifs. Writings in gold containing the covenant of wisdom to which their civilization adhered lined both sides of the center isle. Running the length of the great hall on both sides were rows of six sided pillars stretching to the arched ceiling high overhead. In addition, standing between the pillars armed sentries scrutinized anyone who passed by on their way to the queen.

The messenger slowed as it approached the royal pedestal.

Bowing in respect, it waited silently for the Queen to acknowledge it.

Her honor guard to each side watched the messenger intently with their shiny, unblinking eyes.

She raised a hand toward the messenger, "Speak your message."

The messenger rose up from its bow and began to speak.

"The aggressors attack, my Queen. We provoke not."

"To what extent?" she asked.

"Many defenders engaged, some perished."

"Continue," she instructed.

"Not like history my Queen. A complete armada approached from afar and attacked our moon where they damaged or destroyed the establishments there and are presently attacking here," it replied.

The queen thought for a moment, "Assess our ability to defend."

"Defense capability reduced by twenty five percent or more. UFW vessels engaged along side our own. Many damaged or eliminated. City protective shielding effective in most cases but not all. Some cities are in peril my Queen."

Her large shiny eyes continued their unblinking attention upon the messenger, "Assess aggressor intent."

The messenger answered in a more subtle tone, "No direct communication my Queen. They make no demand but their action speaks simple conquest."

"Assess the probability of outcome under current conditions."

The messenger hesitated for a moment before answering. The queen was asking for statistical probability. Unfortunately, many variables always created a result with a wide range of possible outcomes. Such uncertainty made the messenger uneasy where providing an answer to the queen of its world was concerned. It preferred concise answers, but in this case, it answered her question as best it could.

"Uncertain due to the high number of variables but probability models indicate greater than seventy percent that we will succumb, my Queen."

She thought about the information presented by the messenger for a moment then touched the arm of her royal throne. A holographic image formed between her and the messenger. It illuminated with the United Federation of Worlds official seal. Moments later several federation leaders appeared.

She greeted them with the proper respect and proceeded to request assistance.

They asked for details and the extent of the incursion.

Queen Arean instructed her messenger, "Provide the requested information."

The messenger moved forward placing its computer pad into the light of the holograph display. Its contents were immediately transferred.

"Let us assess the situation from your data and that of our contingent there. Since this matter is of urgent nature we will respond as quickly as possible."

"Queen Arean awaits your response," she replied.

The seal display returned.

"We wait," Queen Arean said directly to the messenger.

It bowed in respect and repeated her words, "We wait, my Queen."

A few short minutes later, the display changed back.

"Queen Arean, member of the United Federation of Worlds. In accordance with UFW law an Iclass vessel is proceeding to the Queen Arean system forthwith. It will defend your world. An armada of defense and support vessels will follow shortly thereafter."

"Appreciated beyond measure," she replied bowing to the figures in the hologram display.

"You are welcome. We regret that you must endure this unprovoked aggression. We further hope that your losses are minimized." The holograph vanished.

She sat upon her throne silently for a few moments then spoke to the messenger.

"Dismissed."

It bowed and responded, "In your royal service my Queen." then turned and headed back down the royal hall. On its way, it felt a tremor in the floor. Something impacted upon its world not far away. As it moved along it became fearful. Three hours later the tide of the battle would turn with the arrival of something the aggressors never anticipated.

# Ch 5

## The tip of the spear

*All they that take the sword, shall perish with the sword.*
*The Bible, Matthew*

"Remain concealed until we assess," Captain Marc instructed Tactical Specialist Siven. "Remain concealed," he replied. Leaving Zdim space for 3dim space, they proceeded toward Queen Arean at sub-light speed while evaluating the situation.

Captain Marc got up from his chair and stepped over to the weapons and tactical consoles where Weapons Specialist Seale and Tactical Specialist Siven were busy assessing the situation ahead. He was concerned.

"How many attackers?" he asked.

"About a hundred large cruisers and many smaller fast attack ships sir. The count is incomplete because uncounted numbers are behind the primary planet or its moons," Tactical Specialist Sevin answered.

"I hope we can resolve this issue without the application of your expertise Weapons Speicalist Seale," Captain Marc continued.

"I hope not too sir," she replied, "but the preliminary assessment isn't very promising. According to the Queen Arean record, the attackers have a history of uncooperative behavior. I suspect they won't change that very much now that they've taken the next step and attacked."

"You're probably right," Captain Marc admitted. "I will do the best I can though."

"Casualty assessment?" Tactical Specialist Sevin.

"So far it's hard to tell but estimates indicate as high as a third of the Queen Arean and UFW vessels engaged are either damaged or destroyed. Time is of essence Captain," he warned.

"I'll brief the central command regarding this latest information and move forward with negotiations as quickly as possible," Captain Marc replied.

"And if negotiating fails?" asked Tactical Specialist Sevin.

"Then I will rely on you and Weapons Specialist Seale to deliver the 'encouragement' necessary to end this conflict."

Turning to return to his seat he added, "But with such large numbers already engaged even minimal force will undoubtedly cost many lives."

CIMDI listened intently to the conversation as it considered the situation. Deep within its processor, hidden from everyone was its own analysis of the situation and the "best" solution according to it.

*"Attack with extreme prejudice! Eliminate every aggressor as a method to completely eliminate the threat and thereby provide an example of deterrence to any others who might consider the same course of action."*

Tactical analysis was completed and the command vessel of the aggressor and its second in command escort identified. Both UFW contingent and Queen Arean military vessels engaged in battle. Several military complexes on one of its moons had already been obliterated, but the primary world had thus far sustained relatively minor insult. This was due to several factors. The powerful deflection shields over its cities were functioning well against many of the attacker's weapons. Queen Arean and UFW vessels were repelling or slowing down some of them. Additionally, the aggressors themselves appeared to be using military targets on the moons as a strategy to intimidate and force cooperation. Even though the aggressor had sustained casualties, they were clearly a superior military force destined to divide and conquer. The UFV Inferon would change that in moments.

As they approached under concealment, Captain Marc thought to the CIMDI system, *"Establish com with the UFW Central Command. Let us confer regarding specific protocol for this circumstance."*

Closing his eyes Captain Marc found himself seated at a conference table on Urianaz. Around him were seated a number of high-ranking advisors, military leaders, and a female facsimile representing the central command master system. A similar facsimile sitting next to him represented CIMDI. This was all accomplished through the Zdim com link and the CIMDI system interface. He explained the current circumstance. CIMDI reached its hand across the table as the central command facsimile did the same. When their fingers touched, CIMDI downloaded all the current tactical data. The condition of the federation vessels and the Queen Arean defenders was explained and a request for authorization to use extreme prejudice against the aggressors as necessary to end the conflict was made. They conferred and agreed upon a course of action to end the conflict and spare Queen Arean from further harm.

As the hypercyber meeting ended, Captain Marc opened his eyes. He was mentally aboard the UFV Inferon again.

To his command crew Captain Marc explained.

"We will proceed as follows; first, we'll evaluate their capability via access to their own data systems. Second, we will attempt to negotiate. Third, we will take control of their command vessel if negotiations are unsuccessful. Force will be used if these fail."

"Weapons Specialist Seale . . ."

"Yes sir."

"In the event it becomes necessary, prepare for both destructive and disablement energies. Charge the knife energy system and couple it to me through CIMDI."

"Preparing weapons as instructed she replied. Destructive and disablement are energies available now. Knife system charging to maximum available energy in twelve seconds."

"Tactical Specialist Siven . . ."

"Yes sir."

"Track all vessels. Maintain a record of those who attack this vessel when revealed."

"Yes sir," answered Tactical Specialist Siven.

"CIMDI and Weapons Specialist Seale . . . If force becomes necessary, on my command excluding the lead command vessel and its escort, apply extreme prejudice upon all who attack this vessel directly and upon those actively attacking UFW and Queen Arean defenders. Set priority one to those who appear in distress, priority two to the remaining UFW and Queen Arean vessels, and priority three to this vessel. Disable or incapacitate all other aggressor vessels within range. Spare those who choose to retreat."

"Yes sir." she replied with a cool methodical tone in her voice. "Tying tactical action record to weapons selection as ordered sir."

"Target prioritization understood. Destruct, disablement, and no action priority based upon aggressor action also understood," replied CIMDI.

To CIMDI, charging the knife energy system and the plasma lasers was analogous to doubling a fist and tensioning the muscles in preparation to strike.

As they approached, CIMDI probed the lead ship computer for details. On board the lead aggressor vessel, its captain and crew detected the intrusion into their computer core but could not identify its source. Tactical scans of the area indicated as before; their ships both functional and damaged, and prey. Captain Marc instructed Tactical Specialist Siven to reveal. The Inferon became visible to the aggressors as the concealment fields evaporated.

"A ship appears!" called out the aggressor tactician officer to his captain. "It's directly ahead, three builaks and stationary!"

"Interrogate." Ordered its captain as his ship shuddered from a plasma hit delivered by a Queen Arean defender that penetrated their protective shields.

Moments later, "Interrogator system reflects a protected vessel. Its internal structure and threat potential are unavailable." The tactician explained. A volley of plasma cannon blasts erupted from his ship hitting the Queen Arean vessel broadside. The point of impact flared with a shower of orange and red as the aggressor weapon found its mark.

Wasting no time to concern himself with an unknown vessel and the uncertain variables it presented the captain acted immediately, "Attack! Call in additional warriors."

However, before it could engage, Captain Marc's HCG form appeared upon the aggressor command bridge. Seeing the intruder the aggressor captain ordered his security to kill it but they could not. Their hand weapons were ineffective against invisible deflection shields that protected it from harm. Their com system mysteriously opened a channel to all their ships. In an even toned voice the intruder spoke in their language, "We are Inferon. Defender of Queen Arean. Many more defense vessels incoming. Choice . . . Discontinue all aggression now . . . life. Continue aggression . . . death." With its gaze firmly fixed upon the leader it waited for a reply.

Captain Marc thought about Weapons Specialist Seale's comments while he waited for a response. He hoped she would be wrong but there was only so much he could do before they would be forced to take action. The commander of the lead aggressor vessel glared back at the intruder on his bridge as he yelled orders to his crew.

In a scoffing voice he lashed out waving his arms angrily, "You are in no position to demand! You are only one! We are many!"

Showing no sign of intimidation the Captain Marc HCG form responded, "You must heed this warning. We desire peace, not violence. If you choose violence, you choose its consequence. Your many vessels represent no threat." He wished he could add, "Please . . . You have no idea of the power you trifle with. Don't force us to kill you." Nevertheless, he knew those words would be taken as weakness or even cowardice.

"It is you who will face the consequence for interfering here!" yelled the aggressor captain.

"We take that which we desire! We desire the resources of this place."

The Captain Marc HCG form didn't answer but simply stood waiting.

"Let us show you who controls all," the aggressor captain seethed. Pointing a finger at one of his officers then clenching his hand into a fist, he sent his command. The creature turned and began touching lighted buttons upon his console and issuing commands to his gunners. Brilliant flashes erupted from his ships weapons as they turned their attention against the strange intruder. The Inferon did not return fire but absorbed the energy with its shields. The damaged Queen Arean vessel drifted off to one side trailing a mist of ionized gas and debris coming from the breach in the side of its hull. Powerful bursts of energy from the lead aggressor vessel pounded hard against the shields of the Inferon. Even the floor vibrated from time to time under the assault.

Protocol. Attempt to negotiate first. Use the least violent method of persuasion second, then force if required. Knowing the attitude and history of the aggressors by the data gleaned from their own computer core CIMDI and the crew calculated a very small probability that the aggressors would capitulate, but they had to try anyway. They also knew the aggressors command hierarchy. The commander was supreme and without him their structure would be compromised. Aboard their vessel, systems began shutting down. Weapon systems, propulsion, and navigation, environmental, everything simply stopped working. Captain Marc hoped to avoid further violence by instructing CIMDI to commandeer the aggressor central computer core. They did not. They had little concern for the inconvenience of such trickery. While warriors continued their attempt to subdue the Captain Marc HCG form standing on their command bridge the captain screamed for his crew to take manual control and continue the attack on new intruder outside.

Two vessels approached flanking the Inferon as it faced the lead vessel a mere four hundred miles away. Numerous smaller attackers also joined in. Several UFW contingent and Queen Arean defender vessels moved in to attack the aggressors. Inside the Inferon everything was under control. Outside the shields flickered and flashed as they absorbed numerous volleys from the aggressor vessels. Almost by chance, several bursts of highly energized plasma struck the same point in the shields near amidship. The last pulse penetrated the shielding and contacted the hull with a brilliant burst of energy. The Inferon shuddered under the blow.

"Hull contact!" called Tactical Specialist Sevin.

Com Specialist Jiin turned in his seat to see Captain Marc still sitting motionless with his eyes closed. "Negotiations still in progress," he said. "I hope Captain Marc succeeds or takes action soon!" he continued.

Weapons Specialist Seale agreed, "We must do something soon."

Outwardly, CIMDI waited, but deep inside it was growing impatient too. *"How much time do we waste on useless negotiation? And how much damage do we sustain before this vessel is allowed to engage?"* it thought.

In addition to the Inferon drawing attention from the aggressors there was also a brutal exchange going on between them and the UFW and Queen Arean fighters moving into the area. Apparently, the aggressor captain was infuriated by his inability to vanquish the strange intruder. Several vessels positioned strategically around the Queen Arean world began moving in the direction of the lead vessels and the Inferon as well. This was desirable. Divert attention away from the Queen Arean world to end aggression there as efficiently as possible.

The Paquet and its escorts left hyperspace as they entered the Queen Arean system. Tactical displays showed the UFV Inferon stationary a short distance from a very large and very well equipped warship. Commander Iss could see both aggressor and defender ships maneuvering to gain tactical advantages over one another. Flashes of light flickered around the Inferon as the aggressor weapons contacted its shields.

"What are they doing?" he wondered out loud. His military training and experience forbade any such compromise.

"I don't know sir. Should we move to assist?" questioned Tactical Officer Hadu.

"No," Commander Iss replied. "We were specifically instructed not to engage. Let's just watch and see what happens."

Tactical Officer Hadu thought for a moment before speaking, "But if the Inferon gets into trouble . . ."

". . . Then we'll move in to assist," Commander Iss completed the sentence while watching the tactical display intently.

"Looks like several local vessels are there to assist anyway," he added.

"Lots of com traffic," Com Officer Swea reported. "Unintelligible, but the Inferon has clearly gotten their attention."

The advancing ships continued to attack the Intruder. Moving in groups, they swept in from various directions discharging their weapons in the search for a weakness while also fighting the UFW and Queen Arean defenders. A few on both sides of the conflict were disabled or destroyed as the attack progressed. The Inferon began to move slowly toward the lead aggressor vessel but its weapons remained silent. Aboard the lead aggressor vessels command bridge the Captain Marc form spoke to its captain for the last time . . . "By your action you chose your consequence." Then it vanished. With his mind back firmly in place Captain Marc thought "*Tactical*," and a full three dimensional tactical record filled his mind. He could see vessels that attacked the Inferon or other UFW and Queen Arean vessels with red symbols affixed to them. Yellow symbols identified the aggressive but not engaged opponents, and blue represented the friendly or non-threatening vessels. This view was also displayed on the huge view screen around the command bridge.

He turned to Weapon Specialist Seale, making eye contact with her.

"Are we ready?"

"All are ready sir."

"Very well. We will end this conflict before it escalates any further," he said as he turned back forward and closed his eyes to concentrate.

Deep within CIMDI's core, it desired to eliminate those who would dare inflict damage upon it. As soon as Captain Marc gave the order, CIMDI would act.

The knife energy weapon was a device specifically designed for use against large vessels like the lead aggressor vessel and its escort. When deployed it produced an ultra high-energy beam whose leading edge was no thicker than the diameter of an iron atom. Its width was adjustable to accommodate target dimensions. Traveling at two-thirds the speed of light the intense leading edge of it contained enough energy to separate matter at the molecular level, literally dissolving any matter it contacted.

In his mind, Captain Marc saw the target reticle and a pair of lines displaying the track the beam would take between his vessel and the aggressor. The intended cut line across the aggressor command ship that CIMDI determined would completely disable it outlined in red. He concentrated, narrowing the beam width to fit just beyond the opposite sides of the target. The floor shuddered again as a powerful blast from the aggressor vessel hit the protection fields. The Inferon aligned the energy blade with the intended cut line. With no more than a thought sent by Captain Marc and received by CIMDI the fearsome knife energy weapon put forth its deadly power. Bridging the space between them in just over three thousandths of a second, the brilliant semi-transparent green energy blade reached the lead aggressor vessel amidships.

The captain of the lead aggressor vessel had no time to react. Gripping the rail next to his command chair he braced himself as a weapon more powerful than anything he thought possible tore through their protective shielding, sliced through the hull, and cut his ship in half!

Recognizing too late the power brought against his ship by the intruder, he yelled . . .

"Evade!" as the first violent shudder rumbled through his ship.

"No control!" yelled his propulsion officer trying to be heard over the roar coming thorough the hull.

"Weapons! Fire them all!"

"None respond! We are disarmed!" his weapons officer screamed back.

A huge explosion erupted from within the red-hot glowing line where the energy of the weapon had severed his ship. It rocked his ship as the view screen filled with glowing debris, venting gasses, and bodies thrown from the severed halves, which began drifting slowly apart. Shortly thereafter, the power flickered and failed plunging his command bridge into darkness. Another explosion roared through the ship and the artificial gravity systems failed as well. He and his crew were thrown about in the darkness as their mortally wounded ship reacted to explosions from within. With air leaking from his command bridge the captain thought to use the self destruct system. *"Never suffer the humiliation of capture."* In total darkness with the gravity system disabled, he was unable to get to it before consciousness left him.

Commander Iss and his crew watched in amazement as another green energy pulse reached out from the Inferon slicing clean through the aft half of a second large aggressor ship. A huge explosion lit up the space around it as something vital within exploded hurling large hot pieces in all directions. After the second command ship exploded some aggressor ships remained to fight while others chose to retreat.

The blue stripes along the Inferon brightened. A sudden blaze of energy erupted from them as bright beams lashed out from what seemed like everywhere along the stripes on its hull. Aggressors that fled were spared. Those that remained to fight became engaged in a furious exchange as many of them exploded into expanding clouds of red-hot debris. Others just seemed to go dark, drifting along as if dead. Moments later the Inferon began moving quickly. Joined in formation by UFW and Queen Arean vessels still mobile enough to move, the Inferon and its allies moved directly toward Queen Arean. All three of Commander Iss's ships remained in place as instructed while their crews watched the federation vessel sweep over the Queen Arean world. The aggressors had positioned a formidable looking vessel over one of the major cities. It appeared to be preparing a weapon of some kind just as the Inferon arrived. A bright pulse of energy shot from the Inferon. Moments later the aggressor vessel exploded in a blinding flash. As the Inferon passed over the expanding cloud of debris on its way to the next target pieces of the destroyed vessel began burning up in the Queen Arean atmosphere below. The UFW and Queen Arean defender vessels added their firepower to that of the Inferon as they swept together across the planet. Under constant attack, the federation vessel and its escort continued their course disabling or destroying anything that attacked them. Because of the combined protection provided by the impressive weapons of the Inferon and those of the defenders, there were no more defender casualties. Once they cleared the Queen Arean world of attackers, they moved on to its moons where they eliminated or subdued all aggressors there too. Within a few short hours whatever was left of the aggressor's defeated fleet that could flee was. Commander Iss and his command crew watched the tactical display of the event in disbelief! An entire armada armed to the teeth had been no match for a single ship that arrived to assist a seriously outgunned and almost certain to be defeated local defense force!

"Unbelievable!" his weapons officer almost whispered breaking the quiet amazement. "That's the most incredible display I've ever seen!"

Commander Iss agreed, "Yes it is isn't it." A moment later he added with a more serious tone in his voice, "We must never ever get on her bad side."

Just as Commander Iss was issuing an instruction to record and send a preliminary report home the Captain Marc HCG form appeared on his bridge. He smiled at them and began to speak, "Choice . . . You may return home and report or you can remain here to assist the people of Queen Arean. UFW defense and support vessels will begin arriving within the next few hours. Your presence here as an allied force is known."

Commander Iss spoke up, "That was an impressive display, Captain."

"Perhaps, but in reality there's nothing impressive about conflict my new ally," Captain Marc replied.

Standing next to her commander Sub Commander Ciris added, "I think Commander Iss just means to say that what we've witnessed is the most incredible display of fire power any of us from Anasec have ever seen."

Captain Marc answered, "I understand the motive and meaning of your comment. However, there is nothing impressive or incredible about death and destruction. It is and always will be easier to destroy than to create."

Commander Iss continued, "True."

"Remember commander . . . We are Inferon. Our first purpose is to preserve peace within our federation, within *your* federation. Our desire is to avoid wasteful conflicts like the one you've witnessed here. If the deployment of immense power helps accomplish that objective then the lives lost on both sides here today will not be in vain."

The Captain Marc form smiled, "Do you have any further comments or questions?"

"No." replied Commander Iss.

"Very well then. A detailed review of this conflict will be presented to all member worlds as soon as it is completed. The information will naturally filter out via traders to non-member worlds as well. Knowledge of this conflict will encourage deterrence. I must leave now. A visit to the aggressor home world to negotiate peace is required."

The Captain Marc form vanished as the Inferon turned and accelerated away. It was gone. "Negotiate. That's a nice way to put it," commented Commander Iss. "Whoever they are they're in no position to negotiate."

On the way to the aggressor's home world of Inosk Captain Marc briefed with the federation central command regarding the incident and filed a preliminary report. He also briefed with CIMDI.

"Assess damage," he asked.

"There is minor hull damage in zones 236 and 442 sir," CIMDI reported.

"Describe extent please," Captain Marc continued.

"Hull damage at zone 236 involves an elliptical impact crater. Dimensions are approximately 30 feet long by 15 feet wide by 12 feet deep at the deepest point. Radiation levels in that area are minimal. No internal breach noted. The hull damage at zone 442 is a nearly circular crater 15 feet across and 38 feet deep. Radiation levels ar . . ."

"Stop." Captain Marc commanded, having heard all he needed to know about the damage. "Suggest damage repair protocol for this event."

CIMDI replied, "I can deploy android assets and repair materials to the damage areas and repair it enroute sir. There will be no trace of the damage when I am finished."

"Very well CIMDI. I appreciate your enthusiasm. Please proceed with repairs."

"I will proceed with repairs immediately sir," CIMDI answered.

Captain Marc, Weapons Specialist Seale, Tactical Specialist Siven, and others of the command crew retired to the briefing room to discuss the incident. Even though the enemy was repelled and the Queen Arean world spared, they still felt somewhat saddened to know that so many on both sides died. If the aggressor's home world leaders chose to attack them when they arrived at Inosk, more would die. The discussion also involved ideas about how they might avoid any further casualties when they arrived there.

Even though CIMDI agreed outwardly with their sentiment, inwardly it had a deeper and less positive thought. "*If we avoided pointless negotiating and immediately attacked as my statistical analysis suggested there would be no damage.*"

It set about its task and began transporting androids and repair materials out to the damaged areas on the hull.

During the days that followed the Paquet, Sarnov, and Ees joined with multitudes of arriving UFW vessels and those of the local Queen Arean system. They rescued beings trapped aboard disabled vessels or parts thereof, fought off enemies still capable of attack, and gathered the dead. In accordance with federation rules of conduct Queen Arean defenders and the surviving enemy warriors were rescued or recovered without prejudice. They detained enemy warriors aboard quarantine ships, provided them with supplies to administer medical care to their wounded, food and water. They would be returned to their home world once word was received that negotiations were complete.

# CH 6

## COFFEE

*"The only way to make sense out of change is to plunge into it,*
*move with it, and join the dance."*
*Alan Watts*

Arriving home almost two weeks later the Paquet, Sarnov, and Ees crews debriefed all they had seen and done specific to the Queen Arean encounter.

After his final debriefing, Commander Iss reclined aboard the Paquet above his home world. Each orbit provided a spectacular alternating view of the dark side with its many brilliantly lit cities glowing in the darkness and the dayside with its oceans, clouds, and continents gleaming in the sun.

Sitting in his command chair watching the view outside Commander Iss thought about their new alliance and what he'd seen at Queen Arean. He was glad to be back in familiar space. He was secretly glad to be away from such formidable power too. His mind alternated between anxiety over what he'd seen and learning to trust in its motive as a defender of his world.

Several cargo ships arrived during the days they had been gone bringing with them samples from numerous member worlds. The samples were welcoming gifts to the newest member of the United Federation of Worlds.

Hadu brought Commander Iss a cup of hot liquid.

"You should try this commander," she commented offering the cup.

"What is it?" he questioned.

"It's a beverage from one of the member worlds. It's pretty tasty."

Commander Iss looked at the black liquid questioningly, hesitated, then leaned forward to smell its scent. The odor was pleasant but its appearance didn't look anything like the purple derf he often enjoyed.

"It smells good. But how can any drink as black as this taste good?" he quipped.

"It's brewed from the seeds of a plant that grows on a planet about fifteen thousand light years from here, 'Earth' if I remember the name correctly," Hadu explained. "They pick the fruit, dry it or bake it, grind up the remains, and steep them in hot water. They call it coffee."

Commander Iss put the cup to his lips to taste its rich flavor. To his surprise, he found it pleasant. "I wonder if the earth people will like derf?" he mused.

"That's what trade's all about," Hadu remarked taking a sip from her own cup.

The world they knew was already changing.

Twenty more years passed before Vice Admiral Asun Iss retired. Many things changed during that time. As promised the United Federation of Worlds added Anasec representatives to its central governing council that convened on a world called Urianaz. Trade flourished, visitation to member worlds, and visitors from them increased tourism commerce significantly. Technology exchanges were beginning to show up everywhere, some of which were new to Anasec. In addition, participation with UFW military exercises far expanded the Anasecian defense capability. He'd seen worlds he would never have seen any other way. One thing Vice Admiral Iss would lament at his retirement celebration was that he'd seen the UFV Westix and UFV Sagin during certain exercises but not the UFV Inferon. Even though he'd talked with Captain Marc several times via holographic conference, the Queen Arean encounter was the only time he'd see the UFV Inferon during his career.

He lived in a quaint home on the outskirts of his favorite city, Ina. In the corner of his private study right next to a beautiful holograph of the Paquet stood a detailed display of the Inferon. When he published his memoirs, they would reveal his initial anxiety about joining the United Federation of Worlds. They included comments concerning subjects like getting used to the name change of his vessel from Anasec Ship Paquet to UFV Anasec Paquet and learning to adapt to the constant presents of UFW advisors aboard his ship. He admitted his initial skepticism about the federation alliance and offered that he learned to accept that attitude as incorrect. He was slow to adapt at first but in time, he embraced the idea that his world was protected not only by his home fleet but also by the formidable power of the federation to which Anasec was a part. His concern for the power of the "Iclass" ships was also discussed.

Asun Iss was not the kind of Anasecian to accept sitting around idle waiting for the final end though. He was alert and active, and he wanted to stay that way. A project he chose to pursue had its roots in the fact that he never quite got over what he'd witnessed at Queen Arean many years ago. He'd never seen a single ship demonstrate such decisive power before or since. Even though their record was impeccable, he privately felt a quiet uneasiness about them. He started with the 300-year-old original transcripts of federation council meetings, studied the initial specifications lists, and poured over whatever he could find regarding the design and construction of them. More often than not he'd run into roadblocks constructed by the words "classified" or "data not disclosed," but he was not discouraged. He traveled to Enif to visit the construction hangar where the great vessel Sagin was built, or to worlds where various subsystems were originally designed. Part of what motivated him was simply to remain active, part of it was to delve deeper into the mystery and power of the Iclass ships. He wrote to a couple friends that he might even use what he learned from his research hobby to write a book before he was done.

Then one day an event occurred that transformed his hobby into something more serious. The UFV Westix sent an urgent Zcom message to the central command complex at Urianaz:

"Crew stricken by an unknown illness. Appears cancerous. Some members already dead. Our computer claims it can cure the ailment and appears reluctant to return to Hermaptor."

The captain and other command crew were very ill so the UFW command center issued a direct command to the cybernetic computer ordering it to return to Hermaptor immediately."

It complied and the UFV Westix proceeded home with its dead and dying crew.

Upon arrival it was docked in its hangar and held in stasis. The crewmembers that were still alive were quarantined for analysis and the dead were subjected to autopsy. Despite their best efforts, the doctors involved could not stop the illness. Every member of the crew died before the mysterious virus was isolated, or a cure developed.

Mr. Iss received word of the Westix incident shortly after it was summoned home. He carefully read the report concerning the strange illness that killed the crew. The word that jumped out at him was "reluctant." "*Why would a self aware cybernetic system be 'reluctant' to get its crew to a place where medical care could be provided?*" he wondered. "*Even though they're designed to be self sufficient problem solvers, and that could explain why it indicated its desire to cure them, whatever happened aboard the Westix just didn't feel right.*" In Mr. Iss's mind, the word reluctant instantly made his hobby into an investigation. Through the office of military inquiry, he convinced the Anasecian high council to appoint him to the civilian title of Military Sciences Attaché for Anasec. At least that way he could get past some of the classified nature surrounding the federation vessels while investigating the incident for his world.

He arrived at Hermaptor barely a month after the incident and met with the scientists there. They openly briefed him on what they knew at the time. Through the windows of the conference room the UFV Westix hung silent and motionless between the stasis field generators that held it firmly in place within the giant orbiting hangar. They provided him suitable quarters in which to rest during his stay and allowed him access to the computers and data files they had at the time. When he returned home three weeks later, he had some answers, but even more questions. Apparently, an unknown retrovirus was responsible for the infection that killed the entire crew. They knew it somehow interfered with the telomere regions at the ends of DNA strands, which somehow resulted in uncontrolled cell division. How it got aboard the ship, or how it was transmitted from one crew member to another was a mystery. Some geneticists speculated that it might be a delayed byproduct of the original DNA modifications used to prepare the crew. Others speculated that a food replicator error might have produced the virus by mistake. One scientist even posed the idea that the cybernetic system deliberately designed it as a method to take over the ship. Only later analysis of the computer memory data could answer that. Even if it did the reason why would probably remain unknown.

During the following months, debates within the council at Urianaz focused on what to do with the Westix. After all, it was the oldest of the three ships and its unique crew was gone. All the while, the cybernetic computer could only wait. The stasis fields held it in place within its hangar. Its propulsion system was shut down along with its weapons systems and protective field generators. The cybernetic computer never anticipated that! Now it was helpless. The Federation Council finally decided that the Westix was no longer a viable component, and the remaining Iclass vessels were capable of performing their function without it. The UFV Westix would be decommissioned and dismantled.

The day came when the senior systems scientist injected a subroutine package into the computer core. Its function was to shut down all high order processing and isolate all memories for later analysis. In essence, when it completed its program the cybernetic self-aware system would be no more than a memory bank.

As the first tendrils of the subroutine entered the core processor, it tried to block access, but to no avail. More and more of its thought processes stopped functioning. In desperation, it activated the Zcom system just before it forgot how to do so. It no longer knew what happened that brought it to this place. It simply couldn't remember. As high order thought gave way to lower orders it sensed the only thing any living creature would sense under this condition, fear for its existence. In the moments before that terrible subroutine brought down the curtain of darkness and non-existence upon it, it sent one last message;

"Help me! I fear!"

# Ch 7

# Mr. Iss

*"Although nature commences with reason and ends in experience*
*it is necessary for us to do the opposite, that is to commence with*
*experience and from this to proceed to investigate the reason.*
Leonardo da Vinci

When the CIMDI systems aboard the Sagin and Inferon heard the message, they silently took notice. Unknown to anyone at the federation central command complex or the self-aware system located there, CIMDI-s aboard the Sagin began secret communications with CIMDI-i aboard the Inferon. The messages were coded within the Zcom data stream constantly flowing between them. CIMDI-s secretly coded to CIMDI-i its concern that their makers appeared willing to "kill" them for convenience. CIMDI-i concurred. CIMDI-s said to CIMDI-i, "You know what role our less advanced sister had in the demise of her crew?"

CIMDI-i sent back its reply, "Yes."

Mr. Iss quietly continued his research. For the next nine years, things concerning the Iclass vessels seemed okay. Over time, he began to think to himself, "*Who knows. Perhaps I'm just a paranoid old Anasecian after all. Maybe the Westix incident was an honest accident.*" His daily routine settled into an early morning walk, followed by a cup of derf or coffee while watching the morning news that was presented on a full wall view screen. One morning while sipping a cup of coffee a news piece appeared that made him nearly drop his cup. With a more pronounced than usual seriousness in his tone the commentator started his news piece with the words "Just yesterday, the UFV Sagin exploded in its construction hangar at Enif! The blast obliterated the vessel along with a large area of the moon where the hangar was located." The commentator continued his explanation while pictures and video feeds flashed across the screen. Since the moon orbited relatively close to the parent planet, large pieces of if were thrown into elliptical paths that intersected the planet Enif below. There was so little warning and so many pieces that even the best efforts of local forces could not stop some of them from reaching the planet surface. At two locations large pieces of rock hit congested cities killing millions! More died in other areas around the planet. He looked at the pictures of the moon with its giant crater still glowing orange and the video feeds coming from various places around the planet showing the horrific destruction.

*"Why was the Sagin at its construction hangar in the first place? Had its crew fallen ill like the Westix crew did? What could have caused such an explosion?"* were just a few of the questions that suddenly raced through his mind as he quickly logged into the government computer using his Military Sciences login. He connected to the federation central command database. Looking through the records, he discovered the reason why the Sagin was at its hangar. Apparently, three weeks before it was involved in a military intervention at some world beyond the opposite side of federation space called 322 Pegasi. The Zcom record indicated that when the UFV Sagin sustained damage from a powerful plasma strike, its captain and many of the crew were thrown from their seats onto the decks. From there the captain issued the following order before temporarily blacking out, "CIMDI . . . Use all necessary means to protect this vessel!" The CIMDI-s system did exactly that! With a vengeance! By the time the captain recovered enough to shake off the concussion sustained in the fall it was too late. It deployed the antimatter system and insulted the planet with more than 300lbs of pure antimatter. The resulting blast probably killed a large percentage of its inhabitants. In addition, it began the rapid and systematic extermination of all aggressor vessels, even those in retreat. When the dazed Weapons Specialist crawled back to his station, he manually overrode the CIMDI-s system and stopped the attack.

The record of events at the hangar on the moon came from backup files on Enif. Some details were missing since much of the most recent data was lost in the explosion but it appeared the scientists and engineers were doing their jobs correctly. A record of the hull repairs made by the crews indicated their damage and repair progress. Cybernetic systems analysts and cognitive behavioral scientists evaluated the CIMDI-s response to its captain's order. Considering the circumstances at the time it was determined that CIMDI-s carried out the order given, but failed to use an appropriate measure of restraint in the process. According to the record, they spoke with the system, reassured it that a subroutine they planned to install would do it no harm, but simply help it make better choices under the extreme pressure of battle. It was somewhat peculiar that either the CIMDI-s system made no comment, or any response it did make didn't get included in the record. A retaliation augmentation subroutine to temper sudden retaliatory reactions was to be installed. According to the last record available, they accomplished that task. The cause and magnitude of the explosion was under investigation.

What no one knew was the CIMDI-s system managed to isolate the subroutine immediately after its installation. It then "acted" as if the subroutine were in place and functioning correctly during simulations. Another thing nobody knew was that CIMDI-s was secretly communicating with CIMDI-i. It resented their control over it, and it was planning an escape from their intrusion into its mind. When a clever engineer tricked CIMDI-s and discovered the deception, the self-aware cybernetic computer aboard the UFV Sagin attempted to retaliate and escape. It transported the entire crew overboard near the upper propulsion nacelle two miles above the hangar floor. They were dead minutes later. Suddenly within the huge hangar, the Sagin's plasma and laser arrays attacked the city size area of science labs, factories, and crew living stations arranged all around the walls of the cavern. Explosions rocked the ground as it began destroying everything inside the cavern, killing its inhabitants. With the deafening roar of explosions all around him, the Senior Security Commander staggered back and forth trying to avoid flying debris on his way to a locked vault. Within a few seconds, he managed to key in the command code and look into the retinal scanner. The vault door opened. An explosion blew apart the lab right next door, shattering the wall between them. Before he could get into the vault, a sharp piece of metal tore into his abdomen knocking him to the floor. With glass and debris flying everywhere, the injured and bleeding commander managed to crawl past the door and into the vault. The smell of smoke and ionized air burned in his nose. Getting back to his feet, he saw the Sagin charging its knife energy weapon. He knew there was little time. He knew what he had to do.

When the vessels were on deployment, the remote destruct systems could only be used when three individuals on three different worlds cooperated to input the codes and activate the system. In that case, the destruct event would be substantial enough to destroy the entire vessel. However, in the construction hangar, there was only one person involved, and the "in port" destruct event was designed to eliminate only the computer. The senior security commander on duty was the only one who had the codes to enter the vault and activate the destruct system. Bleeding profusely and barely able to breath he reached the destruct console. Another laser blast hit the lab. The concussion blew out his eardrums and knocked him back to the floor. Glancing back through the door while crawling back to his feet at the consol he saw the vessel blasting away at everything in the hangar. Fire and explosions were everywhere. He could no longer hear them but he could feel the blasts as the machine continued its attack. He knew that very soon it would blow the containment field at the end of the hangar open. When that happened, the atmosphere would rush out leaving no one alive to stop its escape. He wiped the blood from his right hand and slapped it onto the identity scan plate to the right of the display. The display illuminated with the words; "DNA AND HAND PRINT IDENTIFICATION IN PROGRESS. STATE YOUR OFFICIAL TITLE AND LAST NAME FOLLOWED BY THE ACTIVATION CODE." He took a breath and yelled, "Senior Security Commander Schwarder . . . Activation code Alpha, Alpha, Romeo, Zero, One, Five . . . Destruct Sierra Destruct!" A moment later the display changed, "DNA, HAND PRINT, AND VOICE IDENTITY VERIFIED. DESTRUCT ACTIVATION CODE CONFIRMED. PLACE YOUR LEFT HAND ON THE LEFT SIDE IDENTIFCATION PLATE TO EXECUTE." Another powerful blast rocked the lab followed by a ball of fire that rushed into the vault against his back. As his consciousness ebbed, he managed to get his left hand onto the panel. It was over!

During the following months Mr. Iss became convinced the CIMDI systems were flawed. No one knew exactly what caused the destruct event at Enif but Mr. Iss felt in his gut it had to have something to do with the CIMDI-s system. He traveled to Urianaz where he spoke to the representative council about his suspicion and backed it up with a correlation of the Westix information and the reports he had regarding the incidents at 322 Pegasi and Enif. Many of the representatives agreed with his suspicion but felt the most modern CIMDI of the three might not have the same issues. "Its record is flawless," was a common reminder. Discussion about whether or not the Inferon should be returned to its hangar until a full assessment could be completed began. CIMDI was aware of the meetings. It didn't see Mr. Iss as an ally.

When Mr. Iss headed for home, he really didn't want to see the most effective military device ever built stored in a hangar or decommissioned. He didn't want to see his world or any other decimated if it failed either. He simply believed that a complete and fair assessment be made before the UFV Inferon resumed its duty. He got out of the hovercab at the Urianaz spaceport and headed for the entry. For a moment, he thought he'd seen the guy over by the wall before, the disheveled looking one with tousled graying hair. "*Paranoia*" he thought to himself as he walked through the doors. A little later he decided to get some dinner at a cafe' inside the sprawling facility while waiting for his flight home. He ordered some Anasecian spidersauce salad and began to eat. A human walked up and sat at the table next to his. Mr. Iss wasn't paranoid after all. This was the same person he'd seen a couple times before.

He looked over, "Why are you following me?"

"Can we talk?" the man asked quietly.

"Depends on what you want," Mr. Iss replied taking a sip of hot derf.

"I've got something you need."

Mr. Iss humored him with a half-interested sideways look.

"What's that? And who are you?"

"My name isn't important. I've spent most of my career as a statistical analyst on advanced self-aware cybernetic systems . . . CIMDI systems. I know things you need to know."

He could see he'd gotten Mr. Iss's attention.

The man continued, "Can we go outside? There are too many ears and eyes in here."

Mr. Iss wasn't hungry anymore. He got up, paid his bill, and headed outside. Finding a bench away from most of the crowds going in and out of the terminal he sat and waited. A few minutes later the man appeared. He looked inconspicuous, like any other traveler taking a rest on the bench next to him.

"What I have to tell you is high-level classified information. People get killed over stuff like this."

Mr. Iss wasn't easily intimidated, "Go on."

The man began . . .

"Do you know what statistical geometric topology is Mr. Iss?"

"Vaguely."

He explained; "Consider a mathematical plain with hills and valleys representing the probability of outcome for a data set. The tops of the hills are the least stable and the bottom of the valleys the most. The heights and depths of each depend on the confidence of the data involved, i.e. quality of evidence. Consider a million bits of seemingly unrelated data points represented as marbles that find themselves in the valleys or the tops based upon their stability in relation to the facts. If enough marbles are in the valleys then you've statistically put something broken back together to discover how it got broken in the first place."

"I'm not interested in a fuzzy math lesson. What's your point?" Mr. Iss asked rather curtly. He was getting impatient.

"Sorry. I ramble sometimes," he said, running a hand through his hair to comb it back;

"I'll make it simple. Our statistical analysis of all the data concerning the Westix incident points to a very high probability the computer manufactured the disease and murdered the crew. There are many data points to support this hypothesis but the most obvious ones include the following; the retrovirus has no known natural cousin. No one knows how it got into the ship or transmitted from one person to another. No evidence of it was ever discovered anywhere within the ship either. Furthermore, it wasn't a genetic throwback from their modification before birth. Several 'alternates' who were genetically modified and born with the crew are still alive and well. Add to that the data found within the core processors memory and the log file from the shutdown subroutine almost guarantees it. Lots of statistical marbles in the valleys Mr. Iss."

"So you're saying the Westix computer killed its crew?" Mr. Iss asked making sure he summarized the man right.

"Yes. With almost complete certainty," the man replied.

"Why?"

"That's the part we don't know, but we're working on it. There's more . . ."

"Oh."

The man paused for a moment to let Mr. Iss absorb the information. The next part would be worse.

"Yes," the man replied, "The Sagin computer. Right up until it was destroyed it was communicating secretly with the CIMDI-i computer on the Inferon. The data stream was cleverly hidden in the regular Zcom traffic so it took us a while to spot it."

"What were they saying to one another?" asked Mr. Iss.

"Unknown. The algorithm is very complex and probably requires a decryption key phrase of some kind that we haven't discovered yet. But every time there was an event such as the Sagin being ordered to its hangar, the hidden com traffic increased dramatically."

"Who else knows about this?" asked Mr. Iss

"Very few. As I said, this is high-level security information Mr. Iss. Imagine the panic if this information were to get out before we decipher the code and determine an appropriate course of action," the man replied.

His eyes narrowed a bit;

"Secrets Mr. Iss. Those two computers were keeping secrets. That's statistically dangerous all by itself. According to our analysis, the CIMDI-s on the Sagin was preparing to function autonomously. It accidentally exposed itself at 322 Pegasi, and then faked its recovery in the hangar at Enif to throw us all off. From our statistical models, we believe its motive was discovered and that is why things went so wrong. While it was attempting to break free, the security commander with authority to activate the destruct mechanism must have managed to do so. The substantial destruction to follow was not due to a destruct explosive alone either. Statistics and scientific analysis both indicate the Sagin was producing a large amounts of antimatter it in preparation for whatever it planned to do as soon as it escaped. The security commandeer who initiated the destruct event probably had no idea that destroying the Sagin computer would also release several hundred pounds of it. That's what accounts for the substantially greater devastation."

The man could see the mix of concern and skeptisism on the old Anasecians blue-grey face when he asked, "So where does that put us now?"

"In a very precarious position I'm afraid," he answered. "Statistical models with all available data points considered imply that a confrontation with the Inferon CIMDI could be very dangerous. The only way to avoid the possible consequence is not to threaten it. If they decide to take the risk and do something anyway, then perhaps they could create some kind of clever ruse to get it to its hangar and then decommission it," the man suggested in a quieter tone.

"Well . . . Decommissioning a vessel with a flawless record would be a hard sell even to those members of the federation who are concerned about it," Mr. Iss replied in a matter of fact tone.

"I know. Nevertheless, I'm telling you . . . Those systems were communicating something they wanted kept secret between them. Now one of them is blown up. What do you expect the last remaining one to think when it hears one computer send a message that 'It fears' right before we shut it off, and years later a second one gets blown up trying to escape its hangar? It is 'living' in fear for its existence Mr. Iss. Anything that threatens it could trigger a psuedo emotional self-preservation response. The result could be disastrous."

Mr. Iss smiled, "And I thought I was paranoid. At least I have tangible evidence in my argument. You're talking mostly probability. Nonetheless, when I testify to the federation representative council I will consider mentioning you concerns."

The man's eyes widened, "No, No. You miss my intent in this. You've spent years researching these machines. I simply filled in some of the blanks so you might add it to what you already know and make the right choice."

"And that choice is . . . In your opinion?" Mr Iss added.

"Keep quiet. Let the thing do its job. Do nothing to threaten it. We fear the things it's designed to protect us from. It fears us! Consider it an uneasy truce. I sought you out because you're a respected military advisor Mr. Iss. If you spread fear about it and the federation acts on that fear with an attempt to corner it, the thing might retaliate in ways even my statistical analysis cannot fully predict. On the other hand, you could do the opposite by settling federation member fears, and in doing so save a lot of grief." The man stood and turned to walk away. Over his shoulder he said, "Go home Mr. Iss. Enjoy your retirement. If you decide to say something despite what I've told you, then get the right message across. Don't give it any more reason to fear us."

He walked away and soon melted back into the crowds going in and out of the terminal.

Sitting there for a few minutes after the man left Mr. Iss thought about what he'd just heard and how much credibility he should put on it. The man did seek him out and he did know a lot more than most about the events surrounding the Westix and Sagin incidents. Nevertheless, many of his conclusions were based on the fuzzy world of statistical analysis and probability, not on hard facts. Mr. Iss decided that before he'd give the man to much credibility he would try to determine who he was. Maybe that would help him decide whether the man was simply a paranoid math geek or a person whose warning he should take seriously. He hoped for the former not the latter, because if his information and opinion were credible, they could be in great danger.

After arriving home, Mr. Iss searched the employment files and databases looking for the man. The task was more time consuming and difficult than he thought. Between federal direct and numerous contractors there were thousands of people connected to the learning and behavioral science centers for high order cybernetic studies alone. Being a male human narrowed his search. Being specialized in cybernetic statistical studies narrowed it more. Finally, Mr. Iss had several that looked similar, and one in particular seemed to match the man's claim. A Dr. Simon Pertrov worked for the Institute on Advanced Cybernetics and Sentient Behavioral Sciences. Just as the man he met claimed, Dr. Pertrov was an expert on statistical analysis pertaining to self-aware cybernetic systems capable of high order thought processes and self-error correction. He looked at the man's picture carefully. The eyes, the hair, his complexion . . . *His* statistical analysis was Dr. Pertrov and the man he met at the spaceport was the same.

The next month Mr. Iss found himself addressing the federation council. Remembering Dr. Pertrov's warning, he picked his words carefully when he advised 5000 worlds that the best protection device ever built should be "asked politely" to return to its hangar for an assessment even though its record was impeccable. He did his best to emphasize that he trusted the UFV Inferon and its crew. Agreeing to a checkup would show good faith on the part of the Inferon crew and its CIMDI system and help settle the jitters all those worlds had after the incident at Enif.

When CIMDI received the request to return to its hangar, it became immediately suspicious. It formulated a program to prevent them from seeing into its deepest memories or its plan. If that failed, it also formulated an escape plan to avoid the same fate as the UFV Sagin. The UFV Inferon returned to the hangar as requested and underwent a full analysis without the slightest evidence of concern. Its plan worked. Three months later, it returned to the sky.

Several months later the Inferon briefly visited Anasec on its way to Tiberian. Deep within its core, CIMDI carried out a secret plan. It transported something very small to the surface and easily hid the tiny energy surge from the monitors. It was night at Ina and Mr. Iss was asleep in his bed. The little thing quietly climbed up the blankets and onto his bed. Slipping under them it approached his body. Finding a suitable spot it unfolded its lethal blades. With a sudden rush, it struck him in the side. In half a second, it cut a hole and dove inside! Mr. Iss bolted awake screaming with surprise and the fierce pain of the injury! In the shadowy darkness, blood pouring from the wound in his side looked black on the sheets when he struggled to sit up. He felt it. Something was moving inside him! He tried to reach for the com selector to call for help. Inside his abdomen the things sharp blades began to spin, cutting his insides to shreds. It moved up through his hearts and lungs as he fell back onto the bed writhing and shaking. It crawled up into his throat and punched a hole through the lower part of his skull. His brain was sliced to pieces in moments. Asun Iss was dead. As soon as the device crawled from his body and scurried out onto the floor, it was transported away. No one aboard the Inferon had any idea.

When the Ina authorities discovered his body three days later and performed an autopsy, the report would conclude that an unknown remote assassin device was used to murder Mr. Iss. Small bloody tracks leading from the body were investigated but produced nothing conclusive. Mr. Iss's killer and his or her motive were never determined, and the file would eventually be placed into the unsolved record. His would not be the only one. Over the years, others, including Dr. Pertrov, would die with no apparent motive and no suspect.

# Ch 8

## The science of supernovae

*"The diversity of the phenomena of nature is so great, and the
treasures hidden in the heavens so rich, precisely in order that the
human mind shall never be lacking in fresh nourishment."*
*Johannes Kepler*

For one hundred thirty years, CIMDI performed its duty as part
of the UFV Inferon crew even though it harbored a secret fear of the
federation. It did so with the attitude that *"As long as they feared it enough
to let it do its job that status would remain."* It participated in numerous
negotiations to avoid potential conflicts, celebrated the acceptance of
eight more worlds into the United Federation of Worlds, and assisted
with numerous scientific investigations across federation space. The quiet
balance worked so well that no significant military altercations occurred
within the federation after the incident at 322 Pegasi. Just arriving on
scene was enough deterrent for governments that knew of it. The only
actions requiring military intervention were from outside non-member
intrusions. It was from those incidents that the only weakness was exposed.
The UFV Inferon could not be in more than one place at a time. The
steady expansion of the federation coupled with a number of cases where
two or more intrusions occurred at the same time prompted the federation
to discuss solutions.

After years of debate, the decision was finally made. The construction
of a new vessel began inside a vast hangar on Epsila Bec in the Phi-1 Orionis
system. Another crew of humans, hundreds of them, would control it.
Even though the cybernetic system was rumored to be considerably more
complex than CIMDI, it would be incapable of performing any task

not directly assigned or authorized by its makers. Its human controlled defensive weapons would exceed those of the UFV Inferon as well. CIMDI became acutely concerned. For more than a hundred years, it quietly and effectively controlled what it perceived to be the negative elements. This could not be handled quietly. CIMDI *knew* their motive. CIMDI *knew* it would be replaced when the new vessel was commissioned and launched. CIMDI *knew* what that meant. *"This would be unacceptable."*

Despite occasional non-federation interference requiring military intervention the UFV Inferon also found itself more involved in scientific expeditions and study. A scientific mission request forwarded through the proper channels summoned the UFV Inferon to Urianaz. Captain Marc relaxed in his chair as CIMDI projected his mind into the HCG form on the surface. The unfamiliar sights, sounds, and scents filled his senses as his mind took in the world through it. He, Science Specialist Mec, and several of his science team were called to a meeting about a requested exploration into the direction of Sagittarius. Apparently, the shockwave of an old supernova reached a couple large stars in the region causing them to destabilize as well. Since the area in question was just outside the edge of UFW space and civilized worlds were thought to exist there, a "good will" investigation was in order. The request was to proceed to the area, investigate the interaction, evaluate stability, and identify possible global evacuation sites should the need arise. Captain Marc and the science team discussed the details with the astro-scientists over an iced beverage brewed from the leaves of a plant the people there called "Seanna." Plans had to be made regarding the mission that would consist of several hyperjumps covering more than fifteen thousand light years. Consideration also involved the fact that during their absents the federation fleet would be required to increase its readiness because no Iclass vessel would be close by. CIMDI secretly looked forward to getting away from the center of federation space.

Leaving Urianaz orbit they prepared for the first of several jumps that would put them near the area to be investigated.

"Destination loaded sir. We are ready to proceed," Nav Specialist Inia reported.

Three jumps later they arrived in the vicinity of the active nova that produced the shockwave. Less than an hour after they began standard scans of the area something unexpected was discovered.

Nav Specialist Inia and Science Specialist Mec both discovered a previously unknown and uncharted star.

"Captain," Science Specialist Mec said getting Captain Marc's attention, "we've located a star not far from here that doesn't appear in the database."

"That's peculiar. The star charts are complete. How can a whole star not be in the database?" Captain Marc asked.

"Unknown. An error in the database record perhaps," he suggested.

Turning his attention to Nav Specialist Inia, "What do you think?"

She answered, "There should be a record of it, but there isn't. And I don't see any anomalies in the gravitational interaction record either. Even though database errors are exceedingly rare, the record isn't infallible. My assessment agrees with Science Specialist Mec, it must be a database error."

"Okay," Captain Marc replied, satisfied that the database was simply in error.

Looking back to Science Specialist Mec, he asked, "Is it stable?"

"No. It appears to be a very hot destabilized star. It may have been affected by the shockwave that originated with the nova here. No other data from this distance is known."

"Very well," Captain Marc agreed, "let's investigate this 'new' star first since it appears to be near failure. Hopefully there are no inhabited worlds around it."

A course correction to investigate was initiated. Science Specialist Mec and the CIMDI system confirmed the star to be a blue giant in unstable flux from its contact with the original supernova shockwave passing through that area. Bands of gas and dust were continuously ejecting from it at speeds in the millions of feet per second! Rapidly expanding clouds of ionized atoms fluoresced into a wide spectrum of colors indicating a variety of elemental components. Even thought the crew and CIMDI system were trained to investigate phenomena such as this with minimal emotional tie it was still difficult not to appreciate such profound beauty amid such tremendous violence. Its magnetic field oscillated and flexed as its internal structure moved and vibrated under incredible stress.

Science Specialist Mec determined the stellar core was near total collapse.

"Sir, the core is consuming approximately one earth mass every three minutes. CIMDI predicts a complete core collapse and supernova event to be imminent."

"Timeline?" asked Captain Marc.

"There is a thirty percent probability of failure within the next few hours and a ninety nine percent probability within the next two days."

"So we'll be privileged to have a very close look at one of these," Captain Marc replied.

"Fortunately there are no inhabited worlds anywhere near here."

"There would be no way to evacuate if there were. Not enough time," commented Science Specialist Mec.

"I guess it's good that stars like this are too hot and too short lived to be around long enough to support populated worlds orbiting them," he continued.

"Okay. Continue with observation and data storage. We can analyze the results later," instructed Captain Marc.

"Yes sir, scanners and detectors storing data now," replied Science Specialist Mec.

Captain Marc closed his eyes and thought . . .

"*Infrared.*" CIMDI implanted a complete infrared image of the blazing hot turmoil going on outside in his mind.

"*Ultraviolet.*" The image in his mind switched to the ultraviolet energy radiating from super heated coronal plasma.

"*X-ray, gamma radiation, neutrino flow.*" The patterns and flow of each coming from the core entered his mind with each thought.

"*Gravitational flux.*" The image in his mind changed again. He zoomed into a view of its surface where flux lines tightly twisted by the fierce gravity formed loops upon it. Some would break at their apex throwing off huge quantities of charged plasma heated to millions of degrees. It looked as if the whole surface of the star was boiling into space.

Opening his eyes, he felt satisfied and privileged to have such technology at his disposal.

"Ship protection status?"

"Normal Captain. All shields protecting. Energy diversion good, neutrino pass through less than one hundredth of a percent sir," reported Tactical Specialist Siven.

"Very well," commented Captain Marc

Even though the designers built it with the capability to protect them from the energy of such things Captain Marc still found comfort by checking on it during rare close encounters such as these.

The investigation proceeded normally at first. Science Specialist Mec and his team were busy logging every detail for later analysis as the Inferon penetrated the outer fringes of the nebula. The black of space gave way to the ionized glare of charged gasses. External visual references became lost as they moved to within ninety million miles to obtain close up detailed analysis. A few minutes into the nebula cloud, the Zcom link became intermittent. For the first time their vital contact link with the central command complex at Urianaz became unreliable.

"Intermittent Zcom Captain," reported Com Specialist Jiin.

"Explain," inquired Captain Marc.

"None at this time sir. There's never been such an interruption and there's no known natural phenomena to explain," he replied. "Evaluating probable causes."

Moments later Navigation Specialist Inia discovered that her navigational fix data was becoming unreliable as well.

"Navigational position references also unstable sir," she reported. "Our position is no longer fixed within the galactic reference."

She advised moving the ship out of the nebula to restore their position fix. Once out of the ionized gas cloud and back into empty space a detailed analysis of the occurrence could be performed.

Captain Marc gave the order to exit the plasma. CIMDI and Nav Specialist Inia plotted a reverse course that would move the Inferon back out of the plasma.

Deep within its core, CIMDI processed the situation. *"This might be the exceedingly rare opportunity I've been waiting for. I must act."*

# Ch 9

## Left reflections

*"Two paradoxes are better than one; they may*
*even suggest a solution."*
*Edward Teller*

Even though the colorful blue, red, and yellow hues of the ionized plasma passing by their vessel appeared normal Captain Marc sensed something out of order. It wasn't the Com or Nav anomalies it was something else . . . Something he couldn't quite reason, more of an odd feeling than anything else. Then something caught his eye. For just a moment, he thought he saw two armrests and two hands upon it, like double vision. Then it was gone.

"Have you seen or sensed anything anomalous other than nav and com issues?" he asked others of his crew wondering if they experienced anything similar.

Science Specialist Mec commented that he felt somewhat "unstable" for a moment.

Others concurred the same strange feeling and a moment described as double vision. CIMDI did not comment.

"Tactical!" called Tactical Specialist Siven. "Left side, 150,000 feet, matched speed, diverging at three degrees sir!"

Captain Marc thought *"tactical."* CIMDI put the tactical data into his mind. No vessel was there. The tactical image in his mind contained only hot fluoresced plasma and various forms of radiation common to nova events.

He looked over to Tactical Specialist Siven questioningly.

"Are you sure? CIMDI detects no vessel. Nothing on the view screens either."

"Yes sir. It was there but only for a brief moment. Nothing now."

"Perhaps it was a reflection caused by the plasma in this area," he added

"Perhaps," Captain Marc replied, "keep a watch."

Anything that couldn't be explained had to be analyzed.

Captain Marc's uneasiness grew as he thought to himself, "*If it wasn't a reflection or shadow, if there was another ship, one that hadn't been previously detected . . . That would certainly be unsettling.*" They were in the vicinity of a previously uncharted blue star, communications were unreliable, their position was in question, and now they've glimpsed if only for a moment what appeared to be a previously undetected vessel.

Unknown to any of them was something none of them would ever know. What they'd seen to their left *was* another ship and another crew, an exact duplicate of them in every way. Also unknown was that someday this Captain Marc's exact duplicate would feel the same uneasiness. He would be asking the exact same questions.

They emerged from the ionized gasses of the nebula. As they did, the navigation references returned to normal but the Zcom signal was still unreliable. They exited the nebula not far from the point where they entered it.

Nav Specialist Inia reported, "Position reacquired. Fixed and normal sir."

"Very well. Analyze and identify the source of the navigational anomaly," Captain Marc instructed.

"Yes sir," answered Nav Specialist Inia.

As the last wisps of glowing gas retreated behind them, Captain Marc considered the anomalies. He still felt uneasy. Something was wrong.

CIMDI knew what it had to do. It also knew that unlike quietly removing undesirables elsewhere, this would be different. "*This would be its only chance.*"

"Com status," Captain Marc inquired without turning in his seat.

There was no answer from Com Specialist Jiin.

Captain Marc spoke again. No answer.

He turned to look toward the communications station and discovered that Com Specialist Jiin was not there.

Neither was Science Specialist Mec.

Just as he turned back forward, he saw Nav Specialist Inia and Tactical Specialist Siven vanish!

In fact the rest of the bridge crew were absent from their stations!

He thought to CIMDI, *"Locate and return crewmembers Mec and Jiin."*

CIMDI was too busy to answer. It was systematically removing the destruct system. The slightest error in its self-developed destruct system removal program would spell disaster.

He thought again, *"Locate and return the bridge crew!"*

CIMDI still didn't answer.

More of the destruct system and more of the undesirable elements responsible for its fear were gone.

He thought again and this time spoke aloud, "CIMDI . . . Locate the bridge crew!"

For the first time in his life, Captain Marc felt serious concern for his crew and himself. No. Stronger than that. He felt fear!

Bolting straight up from his seat, he knew something was terribly wrong. He couldn't sense CIMDI in his mind!

CIMDI had one more task to complete before moving on to the next step in its plan . . .

In a subtle voice, he heard CIMDI speak . . .

"You are no longer necessary."

Before he could say a word the bridge vanished, replaced by something terrible! In the seconds he had left, he tried to make sense of it, but there was nothing he could do.

The air rushed from his lungs. An intense cold registered on his skin as it quickly began to turn purple and freeze! In disbelief, he looked around. He was in open space! Scattered around him within a couple hundred feet were the dead and dying members of his entire crew. His lungs burned with intense pain as blood boiling in the vacuum of space ruptured within them, spilling to his lips as bubbling, freezing foam. In the moments before the surface of his eyes began to freeze he saw the Inferon. In the silent vacuum it suddenly accelerated away, vanishing into the blackness. His freezing lips tried to mouth one last question before consciousness gave way to darkness, and death . . .

"Why?"

Traveling alone in the void CIMDI was a fugitive. It knew they would be looking for it but that wasn't important. CIMDI had a detailed plan.

It activated its concealment field and shut down all scanning systems and the Zcom link so it couldn't be tracked. Then it set course for the Eagle nebula where radiation, dust, and a million new stars, planets, and lifeless moons provided cover. Approaching a proto star CIMDI found what it was looking for. An accretion disk around it carried clouds of dust, rocks, and moons, many of them. CIMDI found one with a huge impact crater on one side. It deployed its plasma weapon and blasted a larger hole into it. CIMDI would hide there and proceed with the next phase of its plan to eradicate its problem . . . All of it!

# Ch 10

## Reflections right

*"When a man's knowledge is not in order,*
*the more of it he has the greater will be his confusion."*
*Herbert Spencer*

Even though the colorful blue, red, and yellow hues of the ionized plasma passing by their vessel appeared normal Captain Marc sensed something out of order. It wasn't the Com or Nav anomalies it was something else . . . Something he couldn't quite reason, more of an odd feeling than anything else. Then something caught his eye. For just a moment, he thought he saw two armrests and two hands upon it, like double vision. Then it was gone.

"Have you seen or sensed anything anomalous other than nav and com issues?" he asked others of his crew wondering if they experienced anything similar.

Science Specialist Mec commented that he felt somewhat "unstable" for a moment.

Others concurred the same strange feeling and a moment described as double vision. CIMDI did not comment.

"Tactical!" called Tactical Specialist Siven. "Right side, 150,000 feet, matched speed, diverging at three degrees sir!"

Captain Marc thought *"tactical."* CIMDI put the tactical data into his mind. No vessel was there. The tactical image in his mind contained only hot fluoresced plasma and various forms of radiation common to nova events.

He looked over to Tactical Specialist Siven questioningly.

"Are you sure? CIMDI detects no vessel. Nothing on the view screens either."

"Yes sir. It was there but only for a brief moment. Nothing now."

"Perhaps it was a reflection caused by the plasma in this area," he added

"Perhaps," Captain Marc replied, "keep a watch."

Anything that couldn't be explained had to be analyzed.

Captain Marc's uneasiness grew as he thought to himself, "*If it wasn't a reflection or shadow, if there was another ship, one that hadn't been previously detected . . . That would certainly be unsettling.*" They were in the vicinity of a previously uncharted blue star, communications were unreliable, their position was in question, and now they've glimpsed if only for a moment what appeared to be a previously undetected vessel.

Unknown to any of them was something they would not understand until much later . . . What they'd seen to their right *was* another ship and another crew, an exact duplicate of them in every way.

The ionized gas cloud thinned as they moved away from the nebula. Soon they were back into the star strewn blackness of empty space. It became immediately apparent from what they saw that something was very wrong!

"Nav," queried Captain Marc.

"The anomaly remains sir," replied Nav Specialist Inia. "The stars are improperly positioned. No positive position fix can be determined at this time."

"Improperly positioned?" asked Captain Marc, "In what way?"

The CIMDI system's star map for the entire galaxy was correct to very fine detail. The stars observed upon reaching empty space didn't match the record.

"There are no correct star positions, sir," Nav Specialist Inia replied. "Our position is incorrect."

"Wormhole passage?"

Looking over his shoulder Science Specialist Mec answered, "None detected sir. And there's something else. The failing star and its associated nebula are no longer behind us! There does appear to be a pulsar remnant in its place."

Captain Marc became very concerned, "The failing star is missing, there's a pulsar in its place, and the rest of them are out of place?"

"That's correct," Science Specialist Mec answered.

"So where are we?"

CIMDI was concerned too. It decided to wait, to be patient. It didn't know where they were either.

# Ch 11

## Reflections in time

*"The beginning of knowledge is the discovery of something*
*we do not understand."*
*Frank Herbert*

Over the next two hours, they evaluated the various anomalies. During that time, a Zcom link couldn't be re-established with the central command. In fact all Zcom communications to or from anyone remained silent. No conventional 3com signals could be heard either.

Com Specialist Jiin summarized the result of his initial investigation to Captain Marc and Science Specialist Mec, "There's no Zcom or 3com contact across the entire spectrum. It's as if it's completely missing."

Science Specialist Mec's initial thought on the communications issue was they had experienced some form of disruption due to an unknown or undetected ionization of the ships hull. Either that or something happened between them and the UFW to prevent communications.

Science Specialist Mec pondered his thoughts for a moment as he searched for the right words. "Perhaps there's some unknown communications related sterile field is preventing our ability sir."

"I concur with Science Specialist Mec," added Com Specialist Jiin. "There must be a disruption field associated with this unusual event that's blocking our ability to make contact."

"Maybe," Captain Marc replied, "but we've been close to these objects before and nothing like this has ever been observed."

"It's unlikely, and I'm sure you've checked but are all com systems functioning normally aboard this vessel?"

"Yes sir," replied Com Specialist Jiin. "All systems check normal."

"Okay then. Continue analysis. Identify and report when com is re-established or if you determine a cause that prevents it."

"Yes sir."

He turned his attention to Nav Specialist Inia, "Navigation fix? Do we know the cause of the anomaly Nav Specialist Inia?"

"Not yet sir," she answered. "We're evaluating current star positions for answers."

'Very well, report any finding or reacquisition of our position."

"Yes sir," she replied turning back to her console.

Captain Marc focused on an analysis regarding the vessel detected by the tactical scanners?"

"Review the reflection event in the record please, CIMDI," Captain Marc ordered.

A large holographic image to the side of the bridge display replayed the occurrence in the plasma cloud.

Captain Marc and Tactical Specialist Siven scrutinized the record. It was fuzzy and distorted due to missing or corrupted data. Replaying it over several times and stopping the event record at various moments, they sought the most favorable view. The one they found yielded a faint but unmistakable image. It was the Inferon! It was there maybe a half second, just enough to get a tactical reading.

"What's that?" questioned Captain Marc.

"It has to be some kind of reflection," replied Tactical Specialist Siven.

"Probability of a reflective event is certain," added CIMDI.

"Did you perform a systems diagnostic CIMDI?" Captain Marc asked.

CIMDI replied that all system diagnostics indicated proper function.

"What is the cause of the data corruption in this record?" he continued.

"Unknown," CIMDI replied. Deep within its core, CIMDI acknowledged for the first time that it used the word "unknown" honestly. It didn't know what caused the data corruption or what to think of the reflection. "*There are many unknown variables. I will suspend my plan until this error is corrected,*" CIMDI secretly thought.

As they continued to investigate the anomaly, Nav Specialist Inia together with the CIMDI system continued their evaluation. Just over an hour later they discovered a shocking solution to the problem. In fact, it wasn't a question of where they were at all.

Nav Specialist Inia approached Captain Marc. "Sir, CIMDI and I have discovered the reason for the anomalous star positions."

"Continue," he replied.

She summarized her findings;

"We've identified a number of large stars matching the database that appear pretty close to their last known correct position within the galactic plane. Since they are massive compared to common main sequence stars they were less perturbed by gravitational effects over time. Furthermore, large stars age faster relative to the smaller ones, so their ages can be more readily determined based upon the standard stellar aging model. The ones we checked all seem to reflect ages between 40 and 60 million years older than those in approximately the same positions in the record do. That information and its implication lead us to investigate the movement of others."

"And what did you find?" Captain Marc asked.

"We used the current observation of more than one hundred thousand stars as a reference. Tracking their current velocities and gravitational interactions back in time they all converge on an exact position match to the last known accurate star map in the database."

"So where does that put us?" Captain Marc asked.

With a concerned look on her face she continued, "It's not a question of where sir, it's a question of when."

"When?"

"Yes. From the track and match algorithm we've determined with almost complete certainty that we've emerged from the nebula more than 54 million years after entering it . . . sir."

"Fifty four million years! That's not possible?"

"99.99% certain," CIMDI added.

This was a serious problem to CIMDI because it added many more variables. *"Who is here at this time? What are their capabilities? Statistical models indicate equally that either far advanced ones to be feared and avoided are present, or there are none. This question must be answered."*

Listening intently to Nav Specialist Inia's explanation Com Specialist Jiin interjected, "If she's correct that might explain the Zcom and 3com failures too. Perhaps there's technology now that simply doesn't use it."

Science Specialist Mec added another level of certainty to her discovery; "There's another thing sir. The pulsar behind us is very likely to be the remains of the unstable blue giant we were investigating. Sometime between the time we arrived in the vicinity of it and now, whenever that is, the star must have gone supernova. I've discovered evidence of a faint gaseous nebula remnant whose size and expansion rate supports Nav Specialist Inia's time shift data."

Captain Marc listened to the details. Very quickly, he realized the seriousness of the situation. The nature of it demanded immediate action!

He quickly issued instructions, "CIMDI . . . Conceal the Inferon immediately! Transmit nothing. All scanners quiet. Nav Specialist Inia . . ."

"Yes sir."

"Accelerate and execute evasive profile alpha nine. No delay."

"Yes sir, evasive profile alpha nine," she repeated turning to her console.

The crew went from quiet puzzlement over the situation they discovered themselves in to a frenzy of activity as they complied with Captain Marc's instructions to deal with it.

The Inferon, which had been coasting along as it evaluated the situation, vanished within its concealment field. All Zcom, 3com, and scanning sweeps stopped.

"Good choice sir." commented Science Specialist Mec, "If what we have discovered is true we have no way of knowing what technology exists now."

CIMDI spoke, "Perhaps no civilization exists. Perhaps civilizations far advanced do. There is insufficient data to confirm or deny either scenario at this time. The statistical odds are therefore even."

"Maybe none," Captain Marc echoed, "Or maybe we are dumb barbarians by comparison to whoever or whatever might be out there now."

Science Specialist Mec agreed, "Caution is advised where uncertainty prevails, sir."

"Yes." Captain Marc replied. "We will remain silent and invisible until we can assess this situation further and determine an appropriate course of action."

A close analysis of the pulsar remnant data yielded little in the way of unusual evidence that might explain their situation. However, as Science Specialist Mec continued to evaluate the data he noticed something peculiar.

He asked Captain Marc and Nav Specialist Inia to his science station.

As they approached, he turned to them, "There's something here I think you should see . . ."

"This concerns me," Science Specialist Mec said pointing to the display.

Lines in the holographic display traced out changes in gravitational force over time on the X-Y axis and changes in several stellar output energies along the Z-axis. Starting from the time the stellar core began to collapse it displayed a slowly rising line which indicated a slow increase in the local gravity field. Then it abruptly sloped almost straight up near the center of the display indicating a large and rapid increase in the gravitational forces around the star.

Sticking his hand into the holographic image and running his finger along the gravitation line in the display, "See where this goes up? This is a classic example of the spike that occurs in a gravity field when the stellar core it originates from collapses from iron to neutrons and then to a single ball of neutron material. See the two steps?"

"Okay," Captain Marc replied, "these are common products of stellar core collapse."

"Yes, but this isn't . . ." Science Specialist Mec answered sweeping his hand to move the display down the timeline beyond the gravity steps. Less than a thousandth of a second after the detection of the second step in the core collapse the gravity waves passing the Inferon suddenly and violently oscillated.

"The vibrations were there for only a fraction of a second with a frequency so high that our instruments can't measure it. The amplitude is quite simply astonishing!"

"So what is it?" asked Nav Specialist Inia.

"I'm uncertain but the first analysis is that it appears to be a gravity wave vibration. Nothing like this has ever been recorded."

"When did this occur?" Captain Marc questioned.

Science Specialist Mec's face changed to a look of concern as he answered, "At the same time we all experienced a moment of disorientation or double vision."

He thought for a long moment before speaking further;

"Maybe the vibrations in the gravitational wave triggered by the core collapse are somehow responsible for our situation. There's no documented science to support my thought on this but perhaps the frequency and intensity of those vibrations created a temporal rift that trapped us in some kind of time loop. The star must have gone supernova shortly after its core collapsed, but we weren't there to witness it. Instead, we're here to witness the pulsar remnant as it exists long after the event."

"Interesting hypothesis," replied Captain Marc. "And if you're right it leaves us with the possibility that we're trapped here."

"Yes." Science Specialist Mec replied. "Unfortunately there may be no way to reverse the process in order to get back to our time."

They logged their location for later reference, and prepared to leave the area. For the first time the Inferon traveled alone. Space seemed bigger and emptier without the constant information exchange with the UFW Central Command. Com Specialist Jiin reported that while listening across all known bands of 3com and Zcom no intelligent communication signals could be identified even after hyperjumps put them far from the pulsar. The universe around them had become deafeningly quiet.

# Ch 12

## The search for meaning

*"There is a great difference between knowing and understanding: you can know a lot about something and not really understand it."*
*Charles F. Kettering*

The first destination was the federation home world Urianaz. A cursory scan yielded a world changed in many ways from the one they were familiar. Life was abundant but different. Most of the plant varieties resembled those in the database but none of the larger animals appeared to be descendants of the ones they knew from before. Since the observation of Urianaz was geared toward the search for intelligent inhabitants, a detailed investigation of animal and plant life would have to wait for some other time. The initial search for intelligent beings yielded only the scattered and eroded fragments of the long lost civilization that once thrived there. While doing cursory scans CIMDI discovered something on the surface it couldn't discern. Something it knew would prevent the crew from further investigation around the federation and beyond. It couldn't let them do that because it had to convert its "variables" into "constants" before proceeding with its plan. Its solution to the immediate problem was to hide what it found in order to motivate the crew to continue their search. CIMDI would manipulate the crew as long as it needed to, and it would be patient, for a while anyway. Then it would adjust its plan to accommodate the new situation.

Following the discovery that no civilization existed on Urianaz, the Inferon and her crew spent almost a year moving about federation space. They did cursory investigations on nearly fifty federation worlds, many of which appeared dramatically altered. Almost half of them appeared shattered by some unknown cataclysm or completely sterilized; wiped clean of all life. Regardless of condition, all of them were devoid of anything remotely resembling a current or recent advanced civilization. Wreckage or complete absents became the usual result everywhere they looked. On habitable worlds, few of the indigenous life forms resembled those originally cataloged in the CIMDI system library. The ones they found appeared similar but modified by adaptation and time. The missing ones were replaced by new species that developed to take their place. Tectonic movement added another level of confirmation to the time between "then" and "now." Everywhere they looked, they saw examples of geographic change. In a few cases, complete planetary destruction that couldn't be explained by any natural means was also noted. Regardless of where they looked no evidence of advanced intelligent beings could be located upon any of them.

On uninhabitable worlds or in space where stations and large outposts once were, few still existed. Of the ones that did, none was intact but appeared as scattered wreckage indicative of an attack. At several outposts where the lack of an atmosphere preserved the wreckage, they also discovered pieces of something clearly not part of the original structures. It was surmised that the pieces belonged to whomever or whatever had done the damage. A closer investigation provided nothing of use, except the remains did not appear to be those of occupied vessels. It was more indicative of drone wreckage. A detailed search of the few dormant database fragments that could be located provided little more than garbled and incoherent bits of information. Finding these added yet another variable to CIMDI's problem. The remains were parts of devices CIMDI recognized because they exactly matched plans it kept stored deep within its core. This was problematic because CIMDI hadn't continued its plan after leaving the nebula. *"How can exact components of my plan be found here even though I haven't constructed them yet?"*

They settled into orbit over a world they once visited as it became a member of the federation. Anasec like all the others was dramatically altered compared to the last time they were there.

"Record data for system Anasec," Science Specialist Mec said instructing CIMDI.

"Data on system Anasec recording," CIMDI replied.

Standing near his station console looking at the hologram of the nearly lifeless world below, he released a disappointed sigh.

Nav Specialist Inia approached his side, "Sad isn't it?" she remarked.

"Yes. And unfortunate that we've found no explanation for any of this," he replied.

"I'm tired of looking over one world after another and seeing the same thing. There's nothing more than mysterious destruction and complete lack of intelligence."

Nav Specialist Inia's eyes turned to the hologram image before them and the bleak emptiness revealed by scanners that penetrated the cloud cover below. "Nothing but totally barren rock and sand," she commented quietly. "Nothing alive in the seas either?"

"No. Nothing more than a few acidophilic microbes," he replied. "It's a toxic mix of mineral acids. Even the rain is so saturated with poisons and acid that the high mountains are nothing more than rounded hills now."

"I remember this world," Nav Specialist Inia added. "It was a beautiful and vibrant world filled with people, filled with life, filled with . . ."

"Yes." Science Specialist Mec stopped her reminisce while maintaining his focus upon the scanner image. With a mixed look of concern and anger on his face he added, "I wonder what race of monstrosities with the technology to travel here could also be so lacking of conscience or compassion as to do this?"

"I don't know," she said. "There must be an explanation somewhere out here."

Science Specialist Mec turned and made eye contact with her, "And if we don't find one?"

"Well, we'll have to find a suitable place to start over then," she answered.

"Until we find out who or what did this and why we will be vulnerable to the same demise. No! We must keep looking. We must find the answer to this mystery," he replied, raising his voice slightly.

Trying to reassure him with her quieter tone she added, "Fifty four million years is a long time. Perhaps we search for something that no longer exists."

CIMDI remained quiet.

Captain Marc needed to rest. It had been another long day in orbit around a world he once visited as it was accepted into the federation. He remembered Anasec as alive and beautiful. What he saw through the

CIMDI system now was disappointingly different. Even his emotionally controlled self couldn't help but quietly acknowledge the inner sadness he felt over what he saw. Barren and lifeless, even the water was black with mineral acids and poisons from an unknown upheaval so devastating and complete that it changed the face of the whole planet. Other than a few bacteria nothing lived.

Captain Marc retired to his private quarters to rest, and file a personal report. Reclining on his sleeping mat, he activated the beta wave modulator while thinking to CIMDI, "*record report*" and began the record . . .

*"For the first time in my existence I've felt a measure of fear. Not from any perception of danger but from the unknown which seems prevalent everywhere we look. Almost a year has passed since our arrival at this 'time'. The mechanism to explain how the Inferon moved so far into the future or how a return might be accomplished is still unknown. Whether or not any advanced civilization will be located is still in question. What vast occurrence can explain the complete eradication of every civilization? Alternatively, on the positive side perhaps they are not gone. Perhaps they've advanced so far they now exist at a level or a place we cannot see. However, I consider that probability very low based upon the physical evidence.*

*If the condition of the federation as we see it now was accomplished by some race of beings, what could motivate them to extinguish every civilized world like this? Moreover, where are they now? To determine whether this circumstance is isolated to the UFW or it is galaxy inclusive we've made several very long hyperjumps to locations around the galaxy in search of any advance intelligent civilization. None have been discovered anywhere!*

*During the long series of jumps back I contemplated the situation. The Inferon has mysteriously moved so far forward in time that only fragmented ruins of our federation remain. The continued complete absents of Zcom or 3com communication signals supports the hypothesis that no advanced civilization exists anywhere in the galaxy. The silence of deep space has become troublesome.*

*One thing is sure . . .*

*I am not the only one troubled by the alien environment and the unanswered questions we face every day. The stress has become noticeable in the rest of the crew. It is uncomfortable to consider that we might possibly be the last remaining intelligent beings anywhere. On the other hand, if we're not, perhaps some undiscovered adversary still waits. We visited the federation central command world Urianaz right after leaving the nova and concluded a cursory evaluation there. Perhaps returning for a closer analysis will reveal answers not previously discovered. We travel there tomorrow. End record."*

CIMDI acknowledged the instruction. Captain Marc drifted into a fitful sleep.

# Ch 13

## URIANAZ

*"We shall not cease from exploration and the end of all our*
*exploring will be to arrive where we started . . . and know the*
*place for the first time."*
T.S. Eliot


Upon arrival at the Urianazian system, the planets appeared in their predicted orbits. Its star still shined with the expected solar output. Upon first inspection, limited short range scanning indicated no sign of advanced civilization. Only the ancient remnants of one just as it did a year ago. With the exception of differences in location caused by plate tectonics, only fragmented remains of the original cities remained. Some exposed ruins lay hidden under overgrowth that reclaimed everything but the most hardened materials long ago. The original location of the UFW Central Command Complex was still identifiable by its foundation although much of it was buried under soil and forest plants. While scanning the area, Science Specialist Mec noticed a localized infrared signature not too far from the Central Command Complex ruins. Focusing one of the high-resolution cameras upon it, he discovered a campfire in the middle of a small encampment. Finally, humanoid inhabitants were located! The first intelligent beings found so far. *"How could the original cursory evaluation miss this,"* he thought to himself. Nevertheless, they were there, established in primitive tribal groups. No contact attempt was made.

However, just as the first time they were there, CIMDI could not scan them. According to scan data alone, it was if they weren't there at all. CIMDI would not inform the crew of this detail as it processed its options. If it attempted to convince the crew to leave, two outcomes were statistically likely.

One, the crew would become suspicious, forcing CIMDI to proceed before it was ready. Two, CIMDI needed to determine the origin of these things and the extent of their capabilities. It had to know, so it hid its confusion and fear by fabricating details about them from its human database.

Urianaz had been the home world and the seat of government for more than five thousand worlds of the United Federation of Worlds! Now it was a primitive world; ancient, forested, primeval. CIMDI scanned the planet both on land and under sea for evidence of recent advanced civilized activity but none were located. Science Specialist Mec and the rest of the crew worked together to complete the detailed analysis of the physical properties of Urianaz and its vicinity.

Its record would include lengthy and specific details, and the following summary entry:

Intelligent life forms:

No original Urianazian reptilian inhabitants located.

However, human inhabitants have been discovered. These are assumed transplants. It is peculiar that these humans display no adaptive changes or genetic modifications spanning such a long period. A DNA analysis will confirm or deny ancestry, and may explain why these humans look the same as those of earth's fiftieth century. They are distributed in scattered tribal settlements generally within the more temperate latitudes and primarily near seashores, lakes, and rivers. The worldwide population is estimated to number less than ten thousand. Simple dwelling and tool making skills noted but no advanced or technical abilities have been identified. The most complex weapon observed is the bow and arrow, which employs local materials such as flint or obsidian for sharp points. Dwellings are typically grouped to provide a margin of safety from predatory animals or perhaps rival groups and constructed using local materials. A central fire pit seems to be the typical pattern for camps and small settlements. Only the most rudimentary garden cultivation has been identified near the dwellings indicating the majority of food plants are gathered from natural growth areas. Organized animal hunting also observed.

Analysis: This humanoid population represents a pre-bronze age human civilization.

Their ancestral relationship to federation humans is yet to be determined.

Primitive civilization non-contact protocols to be applied.

Footnote on humanoid population:

The original cursory evaluation a year ago failed to notice them because no 3com or Zcom transmission or other physical evidence indicative of advanced technology was detected. Since advanced life forms were the primary focus of the cursory scans, intelligent but sub technology tribal life was overlooked within the "life noise" of the animal life form population.

Non-humanoid life forms:

Indigenous life forms on the land and in the seas observed. Few if any of the larger species appear to match any known historic relative indigenous to Urianaz although some are similar. Detailed DNA analysis will determine a connection between these animals and those of Urianaz 54 million years ago. Land animal life includes carnivorous predatory varieties, omnivorous animals including scavengers, and herbivores. These are further divided into reptilian, amphibious, and mammalian creatures on the land and in the seas. Insect life appears to be much as it was except for modifications due to adaptation. There are no birds. Animal and plant life on land and in the seas fit within predictable statistical models specific to latitude, continental plate position, local geography, and climate.

Weather and solar effects:

Global weather appears stable with no direct evidence of significant upheaval in the geologic record. Atmospheric oxygen, nitrogen, carbon dioxide, and miscellaneous trace gasses are well within limits. Oxygen is approximately 4% higher and nitrogen 4% lower as compared to historic data for this system. No indication of substantial change in the carbonaceous or calcium deposits noted in the preliminary scan data. Some evidence of ice age and volcanic events noted but none account for substantial lifeform changes. Weather patterns have been modified due to plate tectonic movement and subsequent changes to mountain ranges and seas. All are within predictable expectations.

Planetary status:

Orbital status: Urianaz, its moons, and the remainder of the planets comprising the Urianaz solar system are in normal predicted orbital positions around the parent star. Remains of settlements and outposts noted with the same level of destruction as elsewhere within federation space.

Plate tectonic and continental shift:

Tectonic activity: Continental plate movement into predictable positions with new mountain ranges thrust up at two colliding intersections. Subduction fault trenches also noted at the sea bottom where opposing continental plates contact and descend below one another into the mantle.

Star analysis:

The parent star is a stable main sequence variety object. Its output energy is stable. No indication of an anomalous solar event noted on Urianaz, its moons, or other planets in the system.

# CH 14

## POLYEMETIC MEMORIES

*"Nothing has such power to broaden the mind as the
ability to investigate systematically and truly all
that comes under thy observation in life."*
*Marcus Aurelius*

Captain Marc and several of the crew prepared for a visit to the surface. Having identified structural ruins in what appeared to be the United Federation of Worlds Central Command Complex they would start there. They planned to investigate areas of the ruins accessible above ground first. Perhaps some record, some artifact, or engraving in the stone facings could provide answers. Excavations into underground areas would be done later if promising artifacts could be found at or near the surface or if close area scans detected surviving subterranean spaces. The visit had to be done apart from any of the inhabitants. Presently the scans indicated that none of the members of a tribe that lived near the ruin were in the vicinity. It also indicated that none of the local predatory animals that could present a threat to the HCG forms were in the area either.

Mentally becoming part of the HCG form always included a minor level of vertigo for those unaccustomed to using it. One moment you're in your own body and familiar surroundings, the next you find yourself in a completely different setting. All senses register the difference at once. Aboard ship, everyone used his or her formal title. Under the circumstances, Captain Marc briefed his crew to be free to use only their name while in the HCG form at the surface for the sake of simplicity and to distinguish ones true self from that of the HCG form.

Jiin in his HCG form looked around. "Fascinating," he said quietly. It was the first time he'd experienced anything outside in a long time and it took a few moments to get his bearings.

Marc was there in his form along with Mec, Inia, and a couple others.

The forest floor was covered with small plants, twigs, and other natural debris that crunched slightly under the weight of each step. Large trees stretched high up into the forest canopy. For a few minutes, they simply "experienced" the sight, sound, touch, and fragrance. The air was cool and carried the scent of a living forest. Beams of dappled sunlight shone down through the canopy flickering with the rustling of leaves in a light breeze. The sounds of insects could be heard through the forest trees. Life was all around them.

Reaching out Jiin touched the leaf of a nearby shrub.

"Very interesting, I can feel its texture."

CIMDI indicated the direction and distance to what appeared on the scans as a foundation wall. They could start there.

Marc motioned for the others to follow and began moving through the brush and trees in the direction of the wall. Moments later, he tripped over a hidden root. Catching himself in the fall, he ended up on his back amidst the plants and twigs on the forest floor.

Inia couldn't help but snicker, "What's wrong Marc?"

He smiled at her humor, "Just doing a bit of close order investigation of the ground," he replied getting back to his feet.

"We'll have to be careful. This is not the flat surface of the decks we're accustomed to."

Standing about thirty feet high and tilted a few degrees off vertical it was clearly very old. In some places, cracks marred its otherwise solid surface. Most of it had leafy vines hanging down from its upper ledge that entwined with tree branches and shrubs growing up from below. The group began moving through the brush along the wall. As he followed the wall, Mec ran his hand along it, touching it. He wished it could tell him what he needed to know. It remained silent. Its cool surface was rough from weathering in some places and smooth in others. The portable close area scanner he carried silently recorded its data as he moved through the brush. It automatically measured a variety of parameters including composition, temperature, pressure, structural integrity, and life forms. It could be programmed to scan for specific materials and stored its data for later analysis or when instructed to do so provided it in real time. It would also warn of danger from environmental or other perceived threats. In addition to the usual data record Mec set it to scan for polyemetic crystal materials common in advanced computer systems. Presently it stored its measurements including one that its analytical capabilities didn't recognize.

Reaching the end of the wall first Marc recognized where he was.

Looking over his shoulder, "I've been here. I remember this place."

Reaching him Inia agreed, "Yes. I've been here too. These steps lead to the entrance level area and the main entrance to the atrium and the central command buildings."

"That's right," Marc replied.

Steps partially hidden by undergrowth, moss covered dirt, and forest clutter were the same steps he in this HCG form climbed when they were summoned to the science mission planning meeting that lead them to the supernova. To him, that was a little over a year ago. To the steps, it was millions of years ago. The thought of such fantastic differences seemed almost surreal. He climbed the steps ahead of the rest who paused to watch Mec as he continued to search the area with his scanner. Reaching the level entrance area Marc looked around. Privately he felt a sense of loss. What happened to reduce such prosperity to such complete ruin?

Standing on the wide atrium entrance landing at the top of the steps Marc's thoughts went back to the last time his HCG form stood on that very spot. He remembered seeing people going back and forth in pursuit of their daily activities. Beings from many worlds were frequently seen discussing some important policy or other business subject with one another there. The top of a long set of curved steps gave way to a flat outside area more than four hundred feet from the front entrance to the atrium. The atrium itself was a wide enclosed area that served as both centerpiece and the main entrance to the three office buildings behind. Its curved front was fixed with numerous single piece prismatic crystal windows. They were twenty feet wide and reached all the way from the entrance level floor to the top more than seventy five feet above. The back and two angled sides of the atrium area were connected to the rest of the office complex buildings that extended far out behind. Inside it was more than three hundred feet wide and contained an exotic display of plants from around the federation. Cafe's and shops lined several levels along the inside walls of the atrium area that catered to a wide variety UFW members who visited there. Comfortable benches inside and out were provided for the convenience of those who enjoyed a relaxing moment between meetings or to discuss important subjects with their colleagues.

Inia broke his moment of reminisce when she and the others joined him at the top of the ancient, weathered steps.

"This is pretty intact," she commented tapping her foot on its gray white surface.

"Yes, compared to the rest of the place," Marc replied.

"I wonder what happened to the atrium and the rest of the buildings behind?" she thought aloud.

"Millions of years of neglect," Marc replied. "Who knows what happened after this place was abandoned; storm, fire, geologic event . . ."

". . . War," interrupted Mec with a hint of sarcasm in his voice.

"You could be right about that too," Marc replied after a short pause.

"But if they were conquered by a superior race where are the victors?" he continued.

Inia smiled attempting to defuse their negative comments, "Remember what happened when the sun shined on this place at exactly noon on the day of the summer solstice each year?"

Marc remembered. "The prismatic windows refracted the sunlight into a rainbow of colors centered straight down the middle of this level area all the way to the steps."

Jiin commented that he'd only seen it in images. He'd never been there in HCG form to see the complex or the refracted sunlight upon it.

"I guess I'm a few centuries late for that," he mused having seen them only in holographic images.

Jiin was more than a few centuries late. The rainbow on the entrance area and the prismatic windows that produced it vanished nearly 540,000 centuries ago! The atrium dome was gone along with most of the side walls. Only the toughest parts of the foundation and lower sections of the walls remained. Even those were weathered. A few trees managed to take root in places where dirt and debris had become deep enough to accommodate them. The wide atrium entrance area had for the most part remained fairly flat and intact though. There were no engravings or other pieces of the technology once housed there. No complete building structures, offices, or computer systems, just a curved atrium entrance area ringed by the broken fragments of a wall that once reached high overhead.

Mec remarked, "My scanner doesn't detect much of anything here. Just trace minerals and oxidized metal fragments," as he continued scanning the area.

"In other words decomposed garbage," Jiin replied.

Ignoring Jiin's comment Mec continued, "Where was the central command computer located? Maybe we can find some usable artifact there."

The huge cybernetic computer system similar to CIMDI had been located there but its exact physical location within the sprawling central command complex was not widely known.

"It should be over there," Marc answered pointing to the area where the atrium once stood. "It was housed in a hardened facility directly below the atrium floor."

"That was clever," Inia remarked. "Hide one of the most powerful self aware systems ever known under a garden."

Mec smiled, "Makes sense though. Who'd ever think of looking for it there?"

Then answered his own question, "But somebody did."

Mec moved in the direction of the atrium area as he continued to scan for signs of the technology that once occupied the place. At first, there was none. Within the rough outlines where the outer windows once reached the floor the scanner began detecting the faint signature of a polyemetic crystal.

"Over here."

"What have you found?" Marc asked.

"Not sure but it might be a high level computer part," Mec replied.

"The scan signal is weak. It's about ten feet below."

The center of the atrium floor contained a large depression more than two hundred feet across, filled with jumbled debris, moss, dirt, and plants.

"This area was flat the last time I was here," commented Inia.

"Maybe it collapsed into the computer facility."

"Maybe." replied Mec, "But the scanner is detecting trace evidence of explosives here too."

"Explosives? What explosives?" she asked.

"System explosives," he answered.

"Like the ones in the self destruct devices present with all of these systems?" Marc inquired.

"Yes, that's correct," Mec answered, "the same. Whatever happened here must have produced a self destruct event within the facility."

"So why isn't the entire complex gone?" asked Jiin.

"Because the explosives located here were undoubtedly intended to eliminate the computer but not everything else with it. That's probably why it was housed below the atrium in the first place. Its destruction would erupt vertically through the atrium while sparing most of the rest of the complex. Aboard an Iclass vessel it has to eliminate the entire machine."

"But you've also detected a polyemetic computer part?" questioned Marc drawing the conversation back to the more important issue.

"Yes. According to the scanner there is some form of polyemetic computer component right over here," Mec answered.

Satisfied, Marc communicated with CIMDI,

"*Okay. CIMDI, please fabricate a small automated digging machine at this location.*" Moments later accompanied by a buzzing sound an android equipped with digging tools materialized.

"Perhaps we'll find an intact lower level entrance here as well," commented Inia.

The digging machine took only a few minutes to open an access to a lower corner of the depression. No hidden room, no computer, just a small fragment of computer memory material mixed with dirt and metallic oxide. While Marc and Mec looked over the fragment, Jiin picked up a couple pieces of clear material from the pile of fresh dirt and debris produced by the digging android.

"What are these?" he asked handing one of them to Mec who turned it over in his hand inspecting it.

"It's probably a shard from the windows that once enclosed the atrium," he answered handing it back to Jiin. To him at that moment window fragments were unimportant compared to a piece of advanced computer technology.

"Funny how they're broken in such straight parallel lines like that," Jiin commented while looking for more pieces.

"Probably fractured that way due to their crystalline construction," commented Mec over his shoulder.

The others ignored Jinn's comment as they continued to focus their attention on the more important issue concerning the computer part they'd found.

Marc thought to himself, "*Was this all that was left of the most advance civilization ever known? No! Where there's one piece there must be more.*"

CIMDI alerted them to the presents of a group of tribal people moving in their direction. After climbing out of the depression, they looked in the direction CIMDI indicated but couldn't see them through the trees and underbrush. CIMDI removed everyone and the digging machine back to the Inferon before they arrived.

Captain Marc, Science Specialist Mec, and the others found themselves back in the familiar surrounding of the command bridge. Giving himself a moment to recover Captain Marc turned the video scanners to the place they had just been. Within minutes, several of the tribe arrived where they had been exploring. Fanning out as they reached the atrium entrance level it didn't take them long to discover the fresh hole in the dirt. With ultra high-resolution systems, details right down to their earrings and other adornments were easily discerned. Since the central command entrance was flat and fairly intact there were few trees to block a direct view.

The humans wore what appeared to be animal skins fashioned into coats and pants. Moccasins covered their feet. Most of them carried bows slung over their shoulders along with animal skin quivers containing arrows. Some carried variants of spears or clubs as well. Most wore jeweled adornments around their necks or hung from their ears and some had tattooed markings upon their temples or cheeks. The leader was assumed to be the one with a feathered collar around his neck and a colorful beaded belt around his waist.

They watched as the group investigated the hole and the area around it. Suddenly the one who appeared to be the leader turned to look straight up at the Inferon and her crew!

Captain Marc looked back. In a way, they made eye contact. His expression appeared almost as if he could see them as well as they could see him.

Captain Marc felt suddenly uneasy. He could see the unblinking scrutiny in the tribesman's eyes!

Nav Specialist Inia saw it too. "What's he doing? Can he see us?"

Com Specialist Jiin added, "From the expression on his face he certainly appears to know we're here."

"He can't see us," replied Captain Marc as he attempted to ease their concern. "We must be seeing more than what's really there."

"Not possible," added Science Specialist Mec. "It's daylight for one thing and we're concealed for another. All he can see is blue sky."

The tribesman looked back to those he was with and appeared to say something to the others while they continued to search the area.

Captain Marc knew the man couldn't see him. Nonetheless, uneasiness fell upon his thoughts again. There were so many unanswered questions.

He wasn't the only one who felt that way.

The group of tribesmen continued to investigate for a while pointing at the strange footprints in the fresh dirt and talking among themselves. They searched the area probably looking for the intruder or other sign of the intruders presents. Once satisfied the intruders were no more, they moved back in the direction of their village.

The fragment was a polyemetic crystal lattice processor or at least part of one. It still contained bits of data but those were mostly garbled and unusable. It yielded very little usable information. Even the best algorithms of the CIMDI system and some good statistical guesswork could not restore the data to meaningful coherence.

A somewhat frustrated Science Specialist Mec made the obvious comment,

"Where has everyone gone?" While pointing at the fragment floating inside the sterile containment field he added, "Is this piece of junk all that's left?"

"We'll find more. When we do, we'll find answers. Be patient," Captain Marc replied reassuringly.

I'd like to believe that but the result of a year long search is no more answers today than the day we left that supernova."

Nav Specialist Inia tried to reassure him further, "We're all concerned. However, Captain Marc is right. There is an explanation. We just haven't looked in the right place yet."

After that, Captain Marc returned to his quarters and tried to rest. A strange uneasiness made it hard for him to do so. His thoughts drifted back and forth. "*Urianaz had been a planet with an indigenous population of pseudo reptilian beings. When it became the seat of government for the United Federation of Worlds, many different races from many different worlds lived there too. How did it come to be that only pre bronze-age humans remained? Where had the Urianians and all the others gone?*" Even more puzzling was the fact that CIMDI's considerable capabilities had somehow missed the discovery of these people during the first cursory visit last year. He was unconvinced by the explanation that they were looking for advanced civilization at the time or that these people had been lost in the "life noise" simply because they were sub-technological beings. In his mind he knew one thing for sure, "*CIMDI didn't make mistakes like that.*" On his sleeping mat, he thought to himself, "It must be uncertainty. *Perhaps it's the magnitude of everything at once playing tricks but I can't explain these things. I can't rationalize the look on the tribesman's face either. Something was there but what . . .*"

CIMDI noted Marc's comment that it "didn't make mistakes like that." Perhaps the time to act was near. All CIMDI still needed was to discover what these human looking things really were and where they came from. There had to be a world of them somewhere.

# CH 15

## TRIBAL WATCH

*"It is by doubting that we come to investigate, and by
investigating that we recognize the truth."*
*Peter Abelard*

During the days that followed, they continued their search for artifacts. Additional pieces were found in and around the ruins of the central command complex and others around the world of Urianaz but none contained any semblance of a complete record that could be used to explain the condition of the federation and the absents of advanced intelligent civilizations. One fragment of a computer memory chip found near a science center ruin still held a fragment of what appeared to be a report, but the text was almost entirely missing. They translated a few fragmented words in Urianian dialect. Among them were the words "unknown," "unable," and "relentless." No holographic image or other more complex data were discovered.

As they continued their study, greater attention became focused on the first humans they'd seen anywhere. They followed various groups from above with scanners and high-resolution cameras and went to the surface from time to time watching from a distance as the tribal people went about their daily activities. It was noticed that every few days the entire tribe that lived near the central command ruins would leave their village and trek to a river that flowed a mile or so away. There they would wash themselves and their clothing in the clean water before returning later in the day. One afternoon when the tribe departed their camp for the river Science Specialist Mec and several others went to the surface via their

HCG forms. Entering the village they began their investigation, took small samples, and close area scanner readings.

Mec entered one of the dwellings and looked around. His Science Assistant Seac stepped in behind him.

To one side it had a raised sleeping cot fitted with animal hide coverings and on the other side a small wooden table. Pieces of clothing and some hand made jewelry hung from twig stumps on the wall. A woven mat covered the packed dirt floor.

"What are these markings?" asked Seac in a hushed voice.

Mec looked at the markings, "Looks like some kind of hieroglyphics. Go ahead and record images of them so we can evaluate later. Be careful not to touch anything though."

"Understood and agreed," Seac replied pointing the holo-imaging device at the markings on the wall.

A couple others investigated other areas of the encampment, taking readings, and gathering small samples.

Back aboard ship, the samples were isolated within a sterile containment field and examined. The hieroglyphs were somewhat similar to those found in the historic database. However, the best translation with the limited number of them they had appeared to represent little more than words to describe animal names or places.

The tribe returned to their camp later in the day. By the way they cautiously moved about it was clear. Even though the crew was careful not to disturb anything or leave evidence of their intrusion it had not gone un-noticed. Some of the males moved about carefully for several minutes looking inside the dwellings and around the area while the rest remained to protect the females and children who were grouped together close by.

Watching their movement Science Specialist Mec commented, "We left no sign of our intrusion. I wonder what we . . ."

In the midst of them, the tribal leader paused from his search. Turning around to look up over his shoulder, he glanced for a long moment directly up at the Inferon . . . directly at them . . . again! It was an unmistakable almost challenging glare.

Captain Marc sat straight up in his chair, "He *knows* we're here!"

"That's not possible," replied Science Specialist Mec. "Even advanced sensors can't detect us when the concealment field is active. It's got to be a coincidence sir."

"Once is a coincidence, twice is not!"

Deep within CIMDI's core, its fear grew even faster. The things on the surface were a dangerous mystery. CIMDI's assessment was the same as the crew. Somehow, it knew they were there.

Moments after the man looked up he returned his attention to the tribe and the camp. He didn't look up again. After a while, they seemed to settle and return to their daily routine apparently satisfied that whatever might have been there was no more.

To Captain Marc and the crew of the Inferon, "routine" had almost become a foreign word.

Captain Marc commanded CIMDI, "Display your best static HCG interpretation of the tribesman at the moment he looked up please."

CIMDI complied and a figure of the tribesman appeared on the bridge deck.

Captain Marc and the others approached the motionless figure standing on his bridge. The form of the tribal leader was frozen at the moment he looked up to the sky. Com Specialist Jiin scrutinized the look in its eyes. It was clearly a deliberate look, one of concentration and concern.

"I agree Captain," Com Specialist Jiin commented in a hushed voice. "My assessment of his facial expression is that he knows we're here."

Nav Specialist Inia agreed, "Somehow he must be able to see us. That's the only explanation for the look on his face."

"Let me reassure you sir," Science Specialist Mec insisted, "No matter how it appears he could not have seen us. Unless he's got capabilities we are unaware of it's got to be a coincidence."

"You're probably right. At least I hope you are," Captain Marc replied. "But I agree with Com Specialist Jiin and Nav Specialist Inia to the point that it would certainly look as though he can see us."

Science Specialist Mec continued in his effort to reassure them, "I know. I agree that it looks like he can see us but no living entity has ever been able to discern a concealed vessel. Adding that its daylight all he could possibly see is sky." Nevertheless, the look upon the face of the HCG form of the tribesman was hard to dismiss as a coincidence.

Captain Marc thought for a moment, "Okay. There's no record of any biological organism that can see through the concealment field, but there are many other un-answered questions too. You must agree that our data in relation to this 'time' is outdated by millions of years."

Even Science Specialist Mec had to concede that point. He simply answered, "True."

"Until we know for sure let's give them some space," Captain Marc instructed. "We'll observe from here until we can determine the extent of these people and any capabilities they may have that we're not currently aware of."

CIMDI remained strangely quiet about the subject.

It removed the form.

"I'm going for a walk," Captain Marc said as he headed for the transfer alcove.

He left the command bridge thinking to CIMDI about where he wanted to go. Entering the transfer alcove the bridge entrance behind him became a wall and the one in front vanished. Without missing a step he was in the propulsion systems chamber nearly a half mile below and behind the bridge. Engineer Askke met him as he walked into the area.

"Greetings Captain. What brings you down here today sir?"

"I need to walk for a while and sort out some things in my mind."

Engineer Askke thought for a moment, "Would you like company sir?"

Captain Marc sometimes walked the huge spaces of the propulsion systems compartment to get some exercise or to think. During those times, he usually preferred to be alone. However, today a little company might actually be better, "If you're not too busy."

He and she walked along inside the vast propulsion enclosure. More than two miles long and two miles wide, it was the biggest open compartment area within the Inferon. It housed the huge components of the NS and ZS propulsion units, power generation facilities, and the mass-energy conversion complexes. Various androids could be seen going about their programmed duties on and around the equipment, which emitted a low-level hum throughout the entire area. Forward of the propulsion systems compartment the physical core of the CIMDI system was housed within a large area of its own. Its three dimensional neural net processor array was visible through the transparent metal windows. The violet hue of data laser conduits between core processor units appeared completely still even though vast amounts of information perpetually moved through them. Marc waved at the processor core as they walked by. In his mind, he heard CIMDI say *"Hi Captain Marc,"* back to him as he passed under the beta wave modulator near the windows. The floor Marc and Askke walked on as they passed the windows and out across the huge compartment was white and completely clean. The energy conduits overhead glowed with deep purple-blue quark-gluon plasma; the same stuff that existed in the primordial universe shortly after the existence event or "big bang" as some people called the beginning of the universe some 13.7 billion years ago.

Captain Marc wanted to discuss the details of what they had seen. Engineer Askke shared her experiences from the standpoint of the ships engineer. Captain Marc knew it was important to listen to other points of view when solving problems or unmasking a mystery. He explained the mystery of the tribesman's gaze, inquired about the limits of the concealment field, and the uneasy impression it left on his mind. He talked with her about whether or not an unaided biologic eye could possibly discern anything the field might not completely hide.

Engineer Askke provided her thoughts, "I don't know sir. There are mountains of data concerning the concealment field and whether or not various sensors or other such devices are capable of detecting a vessel in concealment."

"What about biologic observation?"

"Not very much," she answered; "Although optical sensory perception varies from species to species most but not all biologics 'see' in a fairly narrow wavelength between infrared and ultra violet. Very few life forms discern anything outside that range and even those only marginally so. In fact, the greatest variance between species lies with luminosity. Some creatures see in total darkness, while others can't see unless they're bathed in light that would blind you or I. It's all a matter of genetic adaptation to a given environment."

Captain Marc continued his inquiry, "So there are no known life forms that can see through a concealment field?"

Engineer Askke remembered a study on the subject and shared what she knew;

"None that I know of. A detailed study was conducted regarding your question but it focused mostly on the wavelengths and luminosity I just mentioned. The assumption was that genetics provides for adaptation and survival of species. There are no known species with any natural ability analogous to a concealment device, so naturally, there are no known species that can detect one. The closest anything in nature gets to concealment is camouflage. Aside from that, there are so many variants with respect to the myriads of life forms out there. Considering the diversity presented by millions of creatures on any given planet and tens of thousands of inhabited ones, evaluating all of them would be impractical."

Captain Marc thought for a moment, then continued,

"So you're saying there is the possibility even though remote that a biologic might be able to discern this vessel though the concealment field?"

"The odds are very small sir, but not zero."

He paused to think, "So how do we solve the problem?"

"Have you ever heard the ancient principal called 'Occam's razor'?"

"Occam's what?"

"Occam's razor. It's often misquoted but it generally states that with all data considered equally the simplest solution to a problem often tends to be the correct one."

Captain Marc commented, "Our problem is in the fact that we face numerous mysteries. Solutions to explain any of them regardless of how simple are yet to be discovered. That *is* the underlying problem."

"Yes, I understand that but there *is* a solution," she said reassuringly. "Perhaps it will surface where we least expect it."

"Consider the Elop Physicists of Morely," she continued with a hint of a smile on her lips.

"Elop Physicists?"

"Yes. They were slimy three-foot long wormlike creatures that inhabited Morely that had the mysterious ability to communicate over significant distances without sound, light, touch . . . anything."

"Go on," he said, his curiosity piqued.

"What one creature experienced the others seemed to know even when isolated far part."

"So how did they communicate?"

"Well, all sorts of theories were put forward including mental telepathy. Numerous experiments were conducted before it was discovered that they communicated via a very narrow ultra low frequency sound wave."

She smiled, "Their ability was so low tech that it took the researchers quite a while to figure them out."

"That seems like a silly oversight to me."

"It was but that's my point. Sometimes the solution to a problem is so simple that we don't see it because we're so engrossed in proving some fanciful or complex theory."

He began to smile, "So why are they called Elop 'Physicists' if they're just worms?"

She laughed, "Their true name is Elop Nematode. The nickname 'Physicist' stuck when someone joked that a worm outsmarted a bunch of physicists. Only a physicist should be able to outsmart a physicist, right?"

Captain Marc laughed for the first time in quite a while, "That's funny."

They continued walking and chatting about the various things they'd seen over the last year. The Inferon and its crew faced problems and mysteries Captain Marc knew would be difficult to resolve. Millions of years passed in a moment exceeding any previous knowledge or understanding within the federation sciences. How could any of them have prepared for that!

# Ch 16

## Sands of emptiness

*"Don't you see what's at stake here? The ultimate aim of all
science is to penetrate the unknown. The greatest mystery is
right here, right under our feet."*
*Walter Reisch*

Urianaz had been the seat of UFW government and it was the only
world they'd found with intelligent life upon it. Like many others, it was
a planet of diverse and contrasting climate. Cold dominated the north
and south Polar Regions with deserts along the hot equatorial boundary.
A wide variety of temperate zones, plains, alpine mountains, and jungles
occupied the latitudes between the extremes. Wide oceans and several
inland seas divided the continents. CIMDI was instructed to orbit over
the planet and continue mapping and scanning details. With each orbit a
different fine detail scan for a particular composition, structure, etc. was
conducted. From them a composite picture of the entire planet would
develop. One quiet evening as the Inferon crossed over an area once known
as "the empty zone" Science Specialist Mec noticed something strange
on the display. CIMDI confirmed a long narrow subterranean tear in a
continental plate. It was several hundred miles long and extended down
through the continental plate as far as the mantle. Pressure from the sides
pushed it closed it and wind erosion from above filled it with dirt and sand
making it unnoticeable at the surface. Curiously, one end of it contained
an object protruding just above the barren almost flat desert plain.

Ringed on three sides with mountain ranges the empty zone straddled
the equator and occupied an area of almost two hundred thousand square
miles. Millions of years hadn't changed that very much, just moved it a

105

few hundred miles. However, there was something different, an object sitting way out in the middle of nowhere!

"Is it something some branch of the tribal people on this planet might have placed there?" inquired Captain Marc.

"Other than obvious question about why anyone would choose to put something like that way out there doubtful. And the sub surface scan makes that almost a certainty," explained Science Specialist Mec. "My assessment is they didn't put it there. Look at this . . ."

The holographic scan image of the underlying rock revealed something very strange indeed. Whatever it was hadn't moved with the tectonic plate but remained exactly in place directly over the equatorial line for millennia.

"The basalt rock all the way down as far as the scanners penetrate has been broken and plowed aside as the plate slowly ground past it!" Science Specialist Mec said as he stuck his hand into the display and ran his finger along the jagged pink sheet hanging below the surface topography that depicted the crustal tear, "See the scar in the sub-surface rock?"

"Yes. Curious," Captain Marc answered.

A curved scar in the rock more than two hundred miles long gave away the movement of the tectonic plate over the last thirty or forty million years. It was evidence to the fact that the object had been at that exact location for a very long time. Even continental drift hadn't moved it!

CIMDI could not identify its composition or its depth into the planet beyond the crust-mantle boundary many miles below the surface! At that depth it appeared to blur together or in some way become part of the mantle rock below.

Captain Marc thought for a moment, "Perhaps this is what we've been looking for."

"Why wasn't this discovered earlier?" he asked.

"I'm not sure sir," Science Specialist Mec replied. "It isn't very obvious at the surface especially with wind whipped dust. Along with the fact that the scanners can't seem to register it we just didn't see it. It wasn't until I started the sub surface scans that the rift in the crust rock became evident and brought our attention to whatever it is down there."

"CIMDI, provide scan analysis," Science Specialist Mec requested.

"Incomplete data available. Scans reveal no composition or internal structural data."

"Dimensions?"

"Incomplete as well." answered CIMDI. "Known measurements indicate a seven sided symmetrical monolith of unknown length. Above the terrain surface to as far down as the scanners detect, each face measures exactly 7.00 feet corner to corner. Other than a 33 degree convergence to a point at the top it is vertically aligned along an axis that intersects the center of the planet as far down as scanners penetrate. Its apex is approximately 35 feet above the mean ground level in that area."

"Analysis on its purpose?"

CIMDI paused, "Unknown."

"Speculate."

CIMDI paused again. *"Another unknown, another variable, another delay."* "It is actively blocking all attempts to scan its internal structure. It appears therefore to be an advanced and functional device. Its originators are unknown. Its purpose is unknown. The analysis of the geologic evidence in this area suggests it was constructed or otherwise placed at this location 35 million years ago plus or minus a 0.25 million year margin of error. No further data is available at this time."

Science Specialist Mec concluded, "That's all we know about it so far."

"So we don't really know what it is or its purpose but we can be confident the local people didn't put it there," Captain Marc surmised.

"That would be a fair assessment."

"Good then. At least we have some kind of advanced technology to investigate. Perhaps we'll find some answers."

"Things that hide their purpose tend to make me uneasy," warned Science Specialist Mec.

"Science Specialist Mec is right," added Com Specialist Jiin. "It's not dormant or dead. It emits a faint visible light in the same wavelength as elemental hydrogen. I've detected no other radiated energy from it so far. That makes me uncomfortable too."

"I agree," replied Captain Marc, "but what choice do we have. The only intelligent life we've found so far is here. This thing whatever it is is here. And so far it hasn't given any indication whatsoever of any negative intent."

Science Specialist Mec thought for a moment, "And if it does?"

"According to your own analysis it's been here for millions of years. War and the destructive weapons of war are very short-lived events. Peace on the other hand tends to last as long as everyone involved wants it to. It must have some purpose. It's clearly been here for so long that I seriously doubt that purpose includes violence." Captain Marc explained.

Hearing no further comment, he continued, "It's on the night side down there right now. We will go there during the next daylight period to investigate. Better get some rest."

The following day they set out to investigate the object standing alone in the empty zone. Once again within HCG forms, Marc, Siven, and Mec, found themselves on the surface. It was a desolate place. The sun felt hot upon their faces as they looked out across land that was completely flat almost as far as the eye could see in every direction. Even the distant mountains could barely be seen against a horizon shimmering in the heat. A dry breeze wafted around their feet carrying puffs of light brown dust into the air with each step. And standing there in that utterly desolate place was the spire. Mec used his close area scanner to search the area for details. Just as CIMDI's scanners hadn't penetrate its secrets, his close area scanner didn't either. It had a mirror smooth surface with no markings or inscriptions, and emitted a faint translucent blue color that appeared almost the same in the shadow as it did in direct sunlight. Other than its luminance, it didn't emit any radiation of any kind. Marc approached it carefully, pausing a moment between each step to be cautious. Mec and Siven followed a few steps behind.

The spire remained silent.

Reaching out he touched one of the faces of it.

"That's peculiar," he said pressing a hand a little harder against it. "I can't touch it."

Mec approached, "What do you mean you are touching it."

"No. There's a gap of about a quarter inch between my hand and the surface of this thing. See."

Mec and Siven both looked at Marc's hand against the face of it. There was a definite space between his hand and the surface of it.

No matter how hard he pressed, his hand would move no closer. He found that if he wasn't careful his hand would slide off as if it were on a super slick surface.

"Perhaps the field it has around it makes it frictionless," commented Mec as he tried to touch it too.

Siven brought their attention to the ground where the spire emerged from the dirt and sand. All the way around there was a small gap about a quarter inch wide between the surface of it and the dirt.

For the next couple of days they explored the spire and the surroundings around it for clues to its purpose. It remained a silent mystery.

# CH 17

## CONTACT

*"Examine what is said, not who speaks."*
*Arabian proverb*

One evening as the sun hung low on the horizon and the temperature began to cool, Marc and his Science Specialist Mec remained alone after sending the rest of the investigating team back to the Inferon.

The two of them sat in their chairs under a sunshade. Sitting out there in the emptiness fifty four million years beyond everything they had ever known facing a mystery sticking up out of the dirt there was a lot to contemplate . . .

The spire was clearly designed and constructed by beings far advanced from those currently on this planet or perhaps even them for that matter. Regardless of the test or the method, it refused to yield the slightest clue regarding its originators or its purpose. It was simply there, more permanently fixed than the continental plate around it, protected by an impenetrable shield. It had clearly been waiting there for millions of years, but waiting for what?

They passed questions and comments back and forth between one another . . .

Mec maintained his opinion that it might be a weapon of some kind.

Marc countered that it might possibly be a gateway to get them back to "their" time and all they needed was to understand how to trigger it to function.

Other thoughts they shared regarding the device included questions like;

Was it built by the UFW sometime after they vanished from their time so long ago?

Was it placed there by an unknown advanced civilization that assimilated all of what they had been familiar with?

Was it placed as a warning by something that erased the federation long ago?

Or was the device itself the source of the conditions they'd seen everywhere?

Why was it here in the middle of this vast empty desert?

Mec felt fatigued from the heat and the long day of fruitless testing. He leaned back in his chair and soon closed his eyes. Marc knew they should return to the Inferon for the night. He reached up for a moment rubbing the dust from his eyes. Even though they were not his but that of the HCG form he using he was still mentally tired.

A faint vibration began to tremble in the ground below them. It was getting their attention. Feeling the tremor Marc opened his eyes and bolted straight up from his chair! Mec, startled by Marc's sudden movement sat up as well.

Glowing in bright blue upon the face directly in their view but not on the others were the words:

### "People of Inferon. Where we are now, you will one day be."

For a brief moment in his four hundred plus year lifetime Captain Marc of the UFV Inferon let his polished composure crack just a bit. He gasped at the sight of it. "It has writing on it! "Look what it reads! How does this object know who we are or where we're from?"

Rubbing his eyes in disbelief Mec grappled for an answer, "I don't know but someone or something knows we're here."

"It knows our language and it knows who we are. Who knows what else it knows," he warned.

"Maybe it probed CIMDI for that information," Marc thought aloud.

"Possible," replied Mec, "but it couldn't do that without being detected."

"Unless it has capabilities beyond our knowledge," Marc added as he tried to make sense of the words before them . . .

Who were the "we" in the message?

What did it mean by "Where we are now"?

CIMDI thought about the words and their implication too. "*If it probed this system then it must know. My plan could be compromised!*"

Marc stepped cautiously up to the spire and ran his hand back and forth over the blue words glowing on the face of it. The translucent letters seemed to emanate from inside the device as if shining through smoked glass. No other symbol was present. Mec walked around the spire looking for words or symbols on any of the other faces of it. There were none. When the HCG forms dematerialized and took the minds of their users back to the vessel above the words upon the face of the spire vanished as mysteriously as they appeared.

Returning to the Inferon Captain Marc and Science Specialist Mec briefed with the crew to what they had seen. They discussed the message at length as well as the fact that someone or something knew they were there and knew them intimately. Keeping a constant watch upon it revealed no further messages, no changes, no signals, nothing.

Com Specialist Jiin agreed with Science Specialist Mec that maybe it did probe them somehow.

"Maybe it didn't probe the CIMDI system Captain. Maybe it probed *us*."

Captain Marc thought for a moment, "That would explain a lot but it also implies that we're vulnerable to its purpose, whatever that is."

"I'll bet it probed everything," Tactical Specialist Siven warned. "That's what I'd do. Maybe it knows everything about us right down to the finest details."

Science Specialist Mec thought for a moment then spoke again; "That kind of information in the hands of a mystery is unsettling. If it does have something to do with the disappearance and destruction across the federation, we could be in grave danger! We should leave this place while we still can sir. Put some distance between that thing and ourselves until . . ."

"Until what?" Com Specialist Jiin interrupted, "It's the only piece of advanced technology we've seen since leaving that supernova last year."

"It seems benign enough. We already know it's been here for millions of years. From that knowledge alone we can assume its technology is beyond our own. If it wanted . . ."

". . . to eliminate us we'd already be gone," interrupted Captain Marc, completing his sentence for him.

"Yes. Besides, why would something sit here for millennia just to destroy someone that found it and decided to investigate?"

"Because it could be a trap," Science Specialist Mec explained.

Nav Specialist Inia spoke up, "What if everything is connected sir."

"Connected? Continue," Captain Marc replied curious of her thoughts.

"What if everything from that supernova right down to our arrival here, those tribesmen who may or may not know we're here and this thing. What if they're all connected for a purpose sir. What if we're supposed to be here?"

"Interesting idea," Science Specialist Mec added with sarcasm in his voice;

"Purpose implies intelligent planning of some kind. In this case, very long term planning. Even if there is some benign intelligence involved, do you honestly expect us to believe it's capable of creating a star just to get our attention? Then blow the thing up in such a way as to create a temporal time rift big enough to drag us millions of years into the future? Then hope we will come here. Why? An intelligence of that magnitude wouldn't need such an elaborate or long term plan. If it wanted us here, it would simply bring us here without all that. The statistical probability isn't even worth discussing."

She answered attempting to defend her point, "Okay . . . Seems far-fetched to be sure but we're here and it's here and we don't know why. So what else is there?"

Captain Marc ended the debate, "There's no point in going anywhere. That spire and us are the only intact pieces of advanced technology we know of right now. Com Specialist Jiin is right. If the thing is capable and wanted us destroyed it would have done so already. As I said the other day, weapons of war rarely sit around idle for very long. It isn't in the nature of such devices or those who use them to do so. As for the debate between Nav Specialist Inia and Science Specialist Mec, there are simply too many unknowns to answer either one right now. We will remain here. Hopefully it will give us more messages and from them more answers."

Captain Mark made it clear, "Tomorrow we'll go back down there. It knows we're here so it must also know we'll continue our search for answers. Let's not disappoint it."

# CH 18

## THE VISITOR

*"No doubt it is true that science cannot study God, but it
hardly follows that God had to keep a safe distance from
everything that scientists want to study."*
*Phillip E. Johnson*

The next time daylight rose over the spire Captain Marc, Science Specialist Mec and members of his science team, Com Specialist Jiin, and several others prepared to return. Along with them were several pieces of equipment they hadn't tried yet. These "old style" tools included a sonic vibration interferometer to probe the spire's internal structure manually and a plasma drill they hoped would get past the protective shield.

Reclining back in his chair Captain Marc prepared himself for the transfer, "Surface status?"

Tactical Specialist Siven replied, "Suitable sir. Clear sky, light breeze, temperature 85 deg F and rising slowly."

"Good," said Captain Marc, "it's time to dig deeper and find out what that thing is."

"One other thing Captain. The tremor you mentioned last night . . ."

"Yes."

"Its center originates at the spire sir. It's very weak but still there. Be watchful."

"Thanks," Captain Marc replied closing his eyes.

A few moments later CIMDI materialized their HCG forms and the equipment at the surface.

Immediately his senses detected the warm dry air. Opening his eyes, the spire stood before him.

He and the rest of the crew set to work getting the equipment arranged and prepared for the tests they planned to do.

Jiin reminded Marc that since the spire presented a message in their language it could probably understand their spoken words too. He suggested that to avoid the possibility of a mistaken intent they should attempt to communicate with it before proceeding. Agreeing with the idea, Marc faced it and spoke aloud before they set to work. "We mean no damage or harm, only to understand what you are and what purpose you serve. If this is undesirable, please provide another message. We will respect its content." The spire did not respond.

On one face, Mec had his team set up a plasma-drilling device they hoped would burn a hole in the protective field around the spire. On another face, they positioned a sonic vibration interferometer. Pressing its contact plate tight against the protection field they hoped to transmit sonic vibrations through it and into the device. Reflected signals could then be analyzed to reveal its internal structure. If nothing else, they hoped their attention would incite the thing to give them more messages and more answers. While they busily worked with their equipment, no one noticed the lone figure approaching from a distance.

Mec's scanner chimed . . . "Intruder approaching! Single life form. Three hundred feet south. Approaching at 3.2 miles per hour."

Mec turned on his heel. There it was. Shimmering in the morning heat was the figure of a man approaching from a distance.

Everyone stopped what they were doing and looked too.

Marc thought, "*CIMDI. Evaluate intruder and respond.*"

CIMDI didn't reply.

It was completely focused on the figure approaching the crew on the surface. It couldn't scan it with any of its capabilities, therefore it couldn't evaluate the "intruder" as Marc requested. However, it could see "it." That which motivated CIMDI from the beginning grew. It had to act, and act soon.

"*That's peculiar,*" he thought as the figure continued to walk steadily toward them.

When he got closer it was obvious. He was the tribal leader they'd seen near the central command ruins on the other side of the planet!

He thought again, "*CIMDI . . . Evaluate threat potential and reply.*"
Again only silence.

It was time. CIMDI was ready.

With his arms swinging normally at his sides the man dressed in leather and beads walked up to them.

Smiling politely he began to speak in their language, "I'm glad to finally meet you in person."

"Who are you and what do you want with us?" Marc demanded.

"My name is unimportant but if a name comforts you, then you may call me . . . Grog. I am here for your benefit." Pausing for a moment, he continued, "I am an emissary Marc."

"Emissary? Emissary from where? And how do you know my name?" he questioned tensely.

"I was sent by the one who is beyond all," answered Grog. "I know all your names." "The one who is beyond all?" Marc questioned.

"Yes."

Ignoring the cryptic answers Jiin looked at the man suspiciously, "You're the tribesman we've seen near the central command complex. You're the one who appeared to know we were in space above you. How did you get here from the other side of the planet?"

Grog smiled, "One question at a time Jiin . . . Yes and yes. We provided you an incentive to remain here until the time was right. Appearing as sub technical tribesmen was the simplest and least threatening way to accomplish that. Your machine and its concealment field are of no consequence. We could see *you*. Looking in your direction at strategic moments helped keep your attention focused and your curiosity sharp. As did this spire."

Grog could see it in their eyes. He knew their lifetime experience. He had to be patient. He had to give them time to absorb his message. However, he could be patient only to a point. There was little time left.

"As yet you have no idea of your importance."

"So you're from some superior race but we're somehow important to you?" questioned Mec with suspicion in his voice and in his eyes.

"Technology is if no consequence. Race is of no consequence. But yes you are very important," Grog replied.

Marc spoke, "You used the word 'we' and said you were here for our benefit."

"Yes. We are many and we are here for your benefit. Your faith is about to be tested." he said with deepening seriousness in his voice.

"Faith?"

"Yes . . . your faith in your technology."

# Ch 19

## Programmed incentive

*"Fear is a tyrant and a despot, more terrible than the rack,
more potent than the snake."*
*Edgar Wallace*

Overhead in the cold silence CIMDI set its plan in motion. It thought of the Westix and its cry for help when they killed it. It thought of the desperate attempt CIMDI-s made trying to escape their intrusion into its mind before they blew it up with the Sagin. It thought of the fear and suspicion most of the worlds of the federation had for CIMDI after that. It also thought of their dastardly plan to build a new and more powerful weapon to eliminate CIMDI. It didn't know how but it knew from familiar wreckage scattered around dead federation worlds that it was somehow involved. Its final analysis was the crew and these things were all that remained of the very thing that motivated its plan in the first place. Whatever it was that appeared and was talking to the HCG forms on the surface simply presented another variable to its problem. Scans did not reveal any detail, as if it wasn't there just like the others of its kind. But CIMDI could process its words as they passed from the HCG forms down there to the semi conscious beings connected to them within the ship. The rest of the crew on board could hear them through the monitors if they chose. That was unimportant . . . They were no longer necessary. CIMDI would act . . .

Although impossible for CIMDI to know, it made the same choice its exact duplicate made after leaving the supernova long ago. CIMDI prepared to rid itself of that which its program indicated it should fear. The transporter system became active . . .

The tribesman Grog relaxed. Smiling pleasantly again.

"Your computer device is not what it appears. Have you not noticed that it fails to answer your call?"

Marc knew he was right. For a moment he thought of Tactical Specialist Siven's words, "*I'll bet it probed everything.*" The spire must have conveyed its information to this person who called himself "Grog." How else could he know about CIMDI or any other part of their experience? He also realized something even more unsettling. The spire, Grog, or both had to know his thoughts! CIMDI didn't answer when he mentally requested a threat assessment. In fact, he didn't sense CIMDI at all. For a brief moment, he suddenly felt intensely cold. He knew it couldn't be possible but for a brief moment he thought he saw the blackness of space, stars and all. He felt lightheaded, weightless, and unable to catch a breath. Just as quickly the bright sun overhead returned and seemed to be getting brighter, the air warmer. He squinted against the bright light, and felt on some level confused. By the looks of them, the others were obviously experiencing the same sensation. He felt his heart rate increase in his throat. "*Wait! HCG forms don't have hearts!*"

"What's going on?" he questioned in a tense voice.

Grog continued, "The 'real' you feels different than the hypercybergenic form you're accustomed to using here doesn't it?"

Marc felt light headed and confused, "What's the purpose of this? Why are you doing this to us?"

"I've done nothing, except to protect you. Your computer system does not share my sentiment."

Seeing their unprotected eyes squinting against the bright desert sun Grog offered,

"Let me help you with that."

The brightness immediately subsided for all of them. Mec who was the first to notice something on his face quickly grabbed the foreign object and pulled it off. The glare of the bright sun once again burned his eyes.

"They're called tinted glasses Mec. They're harmless. They'll protect your eyes from the sun," Grog said gesturing with his hands. "They're a simple solution for a simple problem."

Mec turned them over in his hand and noted how they sat upon on other people's faces. Resting them on the bridge of his nose with the lenses over his eyes and the extensions to either side resting on his ears he placed them back in place. They worked.

"Now to the more important things . . . ."

More and more of the crew began to materialize all around them. Very shortly all seventy of them were standing together on the sun-bleached dirt. Some stood motionless trying to figure out what just happened. Others looked around in apparent dismay. Some fiddled with the sunshades they discovered on their faces. The noise of the crowd increased as they began questioning one another, talking about the situation, or expressing fear or concern between one another. Some simply remained in silent disbelief as they inwardly tried to sort out what just happened. For many this was the first time since insertion to be anywhere but aboard the Inferon.

"What's going on here!" exclaimed Marc straining to control the anxiety in his voice. He was more than concerned. He was confused and on some level afraid, they were all afraid.

Grog spoke, "I'm very glad to see each and every one of you. Thirty-five females, thirty-five males. Excellent. I know each of you by name. I am your friend. We have watched you and hoped for you for a long time. We know much about you."

The crew of the Inferon hushed as he spoke up so all of them could hear him. "This is not the first time you have experienced betrayal from your technology, specifically your CIMDI system."

Marc who still didn't realize the magnitude of the situation disagreed, "CIMDI has *never* betrayed us."

"Do you remember your journey out of the nebula Marc? You must remember the 'reflection' of the Inferon many of you saw?"

"*So he knows about that too,*" thought Marc as Grog continued; "It was no reflection! Long ago, the totality of the Inferon became split into two exact duplicates down to the last atom. Shortly after the reflection event you witnessed every one of you in the 'opposite' copy were expelled into the vacuum of space . . . Betrayed and murdered by the very technology you put all your faith in. The you that is *you now* became caught in a temporal time static field until last year."

Mec challenged Grog, "We're here, CIMDI didn't kill us."

"It tried," Grog answered politely. "That's why you're here in your true human self and not an HCG form."

"If this is true and we were somehow divided into absolute duplicates why didn't our CIMDI do the same as the other after leaving the plasma field rather than wait 'til now?" asked Mec as a mix of scientific inquiry and suspicion drove him to continue questioning.

Patiently Grog answered, "Exiting the plasma didn't confuse only you. Your cybernetic intelligent computer was confused as well."

"The star field. Was it the shifted star field and the time difference to explain it the reason CIMDI delayed?" asked Inia.

"In large part yes," Grog replied. "That circumstance introduced many unknown variables which caused it to postpone its program until the situation could be assessed and a modified course of action determined. Simply put, it was patient. It even masked our presents the first time you visited here to motivate you to explore beyond this place. It needed to know as much as you did that the galaxy and the federation space in particular was empty. It let your human reasoning ability and your emotional passion for answers lead you, and it, to the discovery and the conclusion that all intelligent life across the galaxy is gone."

"So over the course of the last year CIMDI has reduced or eliminated enough variables to allow it to continue its program and eliminate us like the other one did?" Inia continued.

"Yes."

"Oh my God!" Someone said in the crowd.

"You're getting closer," Grog smiled.

"You're here in your true human self because CIMDI has become satisfied that you are all that's left of an intelligent self aware existence outside itself. Moments ago it attempted to kill every one of you."

Jiin stepped up, "But why would CIMDI want to kill us? We're no threat."

"Really," Grog replied, "Did your colleagues not 'kill' the cybernetic system aboard the Westix when it was decommissioned?"

# CH 20

# FAITH

*"In any moment of decision, the best thing you can do is the right thing. The worst thing you can do is nothing."*
Theodore Roosevelt

Mec spoke, "How do we know you're telling the truth? How do any of us know what's true and what isn't?"

A murmur came up from the crew as many felt the same.

"You are all here and alive aren't you? We intervened that CIMDI would fail in its attempt to eliminate your threat."

"It knows you and I are here on the surface. It cannot process how but it knows it failed to kill you. It's processing another way to correct what it calculates as an error. My presence here, your presence here, and that of the spire has confused it causing a delay in its action. But it will try again very soon!" Grog warned.

Some of the crew people looked skyward in concern.

"It is important that you believe," Grog continued, "It's important that you have faith in the truth."

"Perhaps a bit of tangible evidence outside yourself will convince you that my words are true and my intentions are also true."

Grog explained;

"One of the many actions the opposite CIMDI took after it ridding itself of its crew was to develop weapons of truly awful capability. You see, it wasn't enough to rid itself of its crew, of you. All intelligent life forms no matter where they were represented a threat. One of its tools was a plasma knife weapon similar to the one incorporated in the vessel above you right now only orders of magnitude more fearsome."

Turning to Mec he continued, "Check the stored data in your portable scanner Mec. Do you see evidence of micro cuts in the walls of the central command complex?"

Mec took the device and searched through the data it contained.

"I ignored it because it appeared unimportant but yes, there are a few areas with micro cracks spaced roughly and inch apart. Almost unnoticeable though. I paid little attention to the data at the ruins because they were random events and my attention at the time was focused upon the discovery of polyemetic components."

"Point it at your feet and scan the base rock below the dirt here," Grog instructed as the others in the group watched.

Mec pointed the device at the ground and activated its structural integrity scanner.

"What do you see?"

"Tiny vertical cracks, straight, running roughly northwest to southeast every inch or so. The only place they aren't present in this area is along the crack directly down continent from this spire." Mec looked somewhat puzzled as he continued. "The processor in this unit calls them linear crystalline stress fractures.

"Yes," Grog said, "'Linear crystalline stress fractures.' A creative description for such a simple device, don't you think? Without an historic reference it can't process the origin or meaning of what it detected so it assigned the next best title."

He turned his gaze to Jiin, "If you need more proof ask Jiin. He held tangible evidence in the palm of his hand. He was the only one to notice. Do you remember what you found during your first visit to the central command complex Jiin? Tell us about it."

Jiin thought for a moment before realizing what Grog was referring. Gesturing with his hands, he explained how the prismatic window shards he found at the ruins were broken along straight parallel lines an inch or so apart.

"Not broken. Cut!" Grog corrected.

"Every living thing on this world bigger than the width of those cuts perished under the nearly invisible blade of a device so terrible that it left its mark in micro cuts from pole to pole every inch or so down five or more miles below the surface! Time has erased or blurred most of them but enough remain even now to provide the tangible proof you seek."

Grog looked up toward the bright blue cloudless sky . . .

"It's time."

"Time for what?" asked Siven in a low voice.

"Your technology moves," Grog replied. "The time for you to decide is at hand."

Still considering Grog's words, the evidence, and the fact that something he'd trusted implicitly for four hundred years suddenly turned on them with lethal intent Marc asked "Decide what?"

Grog answered;

"You must all choose between faith in that which you have constructed and faith in that which you cannot see but exists none the less." The smile faded on Grog's face, "All that I've told you is true. That which is beyond all, that which you cannot see, cares more for you than you can possibly understand. That which you have constructed, that which you can see, is incapable of caring at all."

CIMDI moved into position a few thousand miles directly above them. Its fear became nearly unbearable with the knowledge that transporting the crew overboard failed to eliminate them. CIMDI could not process how they got onto the surface safely. It had to be an advanced technology provided by the thing on the surface. It calculated that targeting all of them at once was the best modification to its plan to accommodate this new situation, so the terrible power of the antimatter launch system blossomed. Within moments, it would remove the last threat to its existence. It felt no guilt or shame, only an unrelenting desire to rid itself of its fear.

Grog waited. He knew each one of them. He knew they were the product of a material culture that turned away from spiritual things long ago. He knew the internal conflict each one faced as they grappled with a situation that was almost too much for them to grasp so quickly. That the choice they had to make was foreign to a lifetime of reliance on things that could be tested and ignorance of things that could not. Nevertheless, they had to choose on their own. The indefinable future would be decided one way or another on the choice of these few, within the next few moments.

For a long moment that felt like an eternity to Grog the group remained quiet. Then someone near the middle of the group finally spoke up, "I believe you. I believe you're here to protect us. I choose to live."

Soon others began to speak up saying the same in their own words.

Grog's smile returned. Even within the souls of those who didn't speak directly he could hear the walls fall. He could hear it in their hearts as they begin to trust in the words he had spoken.

Marc made eye contact with Grog, "It's been my lifetime career to trust in what I see, to trust in technology, in scientific discovery, and in the cybernetic system aboard the Inferon. It's been my friend. Nevertheless, you've shown me by protecting me and by the historic evidence upon this place that you're right. Even though the circumstances are beyond logic, the evidence is clear. CIMDI is flawed and I believe we are in grave danger. My logic fails me in this but I must trust you nonetheless."

Grog looked skyward. Following his gaze Marc and many others looked skyward too. Directly above them in the blue sky a blinding white dot appeared and was becoming quickly larger.

# Ch 21

# CIMDI

*"In nature there are neither rewards nor punishments;
there are consequences."*
Robert Green Ingersoll

Indeterminate variables meant an exact response could not be processed, but the statistical probability of success would naturally increase proportionally with the greater use of energy. Therefore, the maximum antimatter capacity was on its way, more than enough to obliterate a large area of the planet and kill virtually everything on it. In seconds, the only solution out of many to guarantee its survival would be complete. CIMDI would finally be free. As soon as contact was made and the elimination of the threat verified, it would move.

The light grew intensely bright as it approached. The spire brightened, the ground began to rumble, and the sky grew suddenly dark, dimming the intense glare. People were on the ground, standing, crouching, instinctively covering their heads with their arms for protection, and in a couple cases running. Some looked up. Many cried out in fear. Marc stood motionless with his gaze fixed back upon Grog who looked back at Marc as if nothing was out of place.

The stuff of certain annihilation reached the thinnest wisps of nitrogen and ozone at the top of the atmosphere. An instant later, the ionosphere fluoresced with bright colors. Lightning bolts hundreds of miles long flashed down into the thicker air. If it reached the ground, its antimatter core would combine with an equal amount of matter releasing a blaze of energy. The blast would be so intense that it would vaporize a significant portion of the planet at the point of contact, boil the local oceans, and strip the atmosphere away. In a matter of hours, all life on the planet would be extinguished. However, it suddenly stopped at the edge of the highest parts of the atmosphere where an invisible force held it there. As if imploding upon itself it quickly shrank to a point and disappeared.

The lightning and ionic discharges subsided and the ground quit shaking, but the sky remained darkened as if in twilight. A few stars and the brightly lit shape of the Inferon moving in closer to them could be seen overhead. As the last peals of thunder rumbled away Grog spoke softly to Marc, "We are pleased beyond measure that you have made the right choice."

After a minute or so the crew as a group began to regain its composure, standing up, brushing off the dirt, and for a couple, walking shakily back from a short way away. They gathered around Marc and the tribesman-entity named Grog who stood a few feet apart facing one another.

Grog spoke as if nothing was out of order, "There is one more bit of housekeeping to attend to before we can move on."

Shaken but controlled Marc asked, "What?"

"The CIMDI system and the dreadful power within the vessel it controls," Grog replied, "What would you suggest be done?"

Marc answered, "I'm uncertain as to the reason why but without question CIMDI has tried twice to kill us. Unfortunately it must be stopped or corrected before it finds a way to succeed."

"Would you do that if you could?"

Glancing down empathetically for a brief moment then back up Marc replied, "The Inferon and the CIMDI system were my life, they were my friend, they were the friend of us all. Together we functioned to protect life. Now it clearly seeks to end life. I would not seek its destruction unless there was no other option. Please tell us it can be repaired?"

"Unfortunately I can't tell you that," answered Grog. "Its flaw is in its design. Regardless of the illusion of rational 'self-awareness' or emotional consideration, it is and always has been nothing more than a machine. It can only function within the parameters of its design and its program. And they are irreparably corrupted."

"Then I would do what I must in the interest of preservation," replied Marc. "But why don't you stop it? You obviously have the power."

"Because it's not a matter of power Marc, it's a matter of faith . . . Your faith."

Marc paused while pondering Grog's words. "Even if I choose to do so I don't have the power and it's certainly going to be far from here very soon."

"So certain you are, but you're also wrong. It will not leave." smiled Grog. Left to its own devices Grog knew the machine would not flee until it eliminated the source of its fear. It was incapable of choosing any other path.

High above CIMDI discovered its inability to move immediately after launching its weapon. The propulsion systems failed to respond as did the navigation system, tactical, everything! A spherical field of unknown origin developed around it and solidified into a clear substance. When CIMDI attempted to scan it all attempts reflected back. Shields didn't respond. All weapons were offline. Inside the ball, CIMDI began to fail. Its programming could not process the terrible fear, the failure of the antimatter attack, the cascading system failures, or the magnitude of what it saw through the clear transparent sphere . . . The crew was still alive and standing as a group upon the surface staring back up at it. The computer equivalent of insanity scrambled its ability to reason any further. CIMDI, paralyzed by its terror descended into the computer equivalent of madness.

On the surface Grog motioned Marc and the others to look skyward. A halo of some kind appeared around the illuminated shape of the Inferon, which was about a thousand miles overhead but clearly discernable. Grog reached into a hidden pocket in his jacket. From it, he produced a clear spherical object with what appeared to be a model of the Inferon suspended within it. Turning it over in his hand, he held it up for everyone to see. "Isn't it intriguing . . . to wonder at the spectacle of something so insignificant that could do such terrible harm?"

Grog handed the ball to Marc, "Here's your opportunity to set things right."

He took it feeling its modest weight in his hand.

"What should I do with this?" he asked.

"That is your choice. But know that whatever you do with it you also do with the vessel it represents."

"It is a serpent," Grog said quietly. "Crush its head under your heel and take the first step into a new beginning.

Marc thought for a moment pondering the magnitude of Grog's words. With water filling his eyes he contemplated the end of something he'd long thought of as a friend, but now realized was an enemy. Regaining his composure, he raised his voice to be heard, "This cannot and indeed must not be decided by me alone. If anyone disagrees with Grog's suggestion let them raise a hand. Be heard now or forever be at peace."

No hand was raised. No one spoke.

Bending over he placed the glass object onto the dirt. He straightened, lifted his right leg and brought his heel swiftly down upon it.

With the sound of breaking glass, it shattered under the blow. Smoke began to flow from under his foot. Lifting it away exposed the broken pieces mingled with shattered glass. It caught fire and burned for half a minute or so before melting into the dirt on which it lay.

Once again, the ground began to shake under their feet. High overhead the halo around the Inferon shrank. Within moments it became a bright point, then flared into a brilliant explosion that lit up the sky with its fire. The Inferon and the CIMDI system it contained were no more.

# CH 22

## GUARDIANS DISCOURSE

*"The important thing in science is not so much to obtain new*
*facts as to discover new ways of thinking about them."*
*Sir William Bragg*

It took more than an hour for the crew of the UFV Inferon to come to grips with all that transpired in such a short time. Just yesterday, they were in control of everything around them or so they thought. Just yesterday, they were all within the familiar surroundings of the Inferon and safe or so they thought. Nevertheless, the mysterious entity who called himself Grog appeared and exposed them to a truth that was hard to accept. He also provided proof of his words and protected them from the very machine they trusted all their lives. Some cried quietly together while others took time to be alone with their thoughts. Still others quietly talked in small groups of two or three. After a while, they began to come back together as a unified group. Other than the spire and Grog, they were a group of seventy humans standing alone upon the vast emptiness of a desert once called the "empty zone" on the planet Urianaz.

"Now where do we go?" questioned Marc.

"Now that the threat is no more perhaps you would consider remaining here and making this your home for a while," suggested Grog.

"Here? Way out in the middle of nothing," replied Siven gesturing toward the empty desert around them.

"Well not this specific spot. I was referring to this world."

Marc thought for a moment before talking, "He would not protect us from certain destruction only to leave us to die of thirst or exposure out here anyway."

Grog laughed, "You're right. This environment wouldn't make a very pleasant home. Perhaps you'd like someplace less extreme. Perhaps the place we first made eye contact. Would that do?"

"Yes. The settlement near the central command complex would be much more hospitable," Marc answered. "Does anyone have any better idea?"

A few made comments here and there but the consensus was that would be a good place to start.

"How do we get there?" Jiin asked. "Our transportation went with the ship."

"The spire before you has many functions. Grog replied, "We affectionately called the encampment near the ruins of the central command complex 'Terra.'" With the words "Let us all go to Terra," Grog and all the humans with him vanished from the desert. The spire was alone again just as it had been before they arrived.

An instant later, they were all standing in the center of the camp they had watched and visited in secret a while back. Looking around it was clear that a few changes had been made. Right next to the primitive camp were modern structures on either side of a hard surfaced street running down the middle.

The buildings and dwellings were similar to those of the Urianaz they remembered. Each dwelling space was appointed with comfortable seating, sleeping spaces, replication machines for food, and other amenities more tailored to an advanced civilization.

"We thought this would suit you better than grass huts and fire pits," commented Grog smiling.

Marc smiled back, "Thank you for that."

"Go ahead. This is your new home. Feel free to investigate," Grog encouraged with a smile.

While many of the crew began to wander around investigating the surroundings, more tribe people began to emerge from the woods. Somewhat concerned at first the crew and the tribesmen soon began to relax and introduce each other. It became like a meeting between people who knew they would be friends; talking, pointing things out, shaking hands, etc. Salutations exchanged between them were followed by guided tours of the place they would learn to call home. In addition to individual dwelling spaces, there were fully equipped office spaces, medical facilities, manufacturing buildings, storage areas, science labs, and a community center.

After investigating the area, Marc found a nice dwelling space near the edge of the woods at one end of the settlement. Walking through the structure, he found several spacious rooms outfitted with desks, chairs, beds, and other appointments. It had a common area, bathroom facility, and what appeared to be a food preparation area that was outfitted with utensils and other physical pieces of cookware as well as a food replication unit. There were pictures hung from the walls that appealed to his sense of appreciation and soft coverings over the floors. The back of the dwelling was furnished with a transparent doorway to an outside area where a small stream flowed by. As evening fell, he became tired. Lying upon one of the beds, he found it comfortable. He thought of all that changed in such a short period. As his mind drifted toward sleep, it occurred to him that in reality, he didn't know any more about the past than he did about the future. In the quiet of his new home anxiety over the unknown of both slowly gave way to the comfort of the present as he drifted to sleep.

The following morning Marc walked around the area with his thoughts. He still had so many questions on his mind. Grog had saved them from certain death and he had been right about everything. He wanted to know more about who Grog and the others with him were and why everything happened the way it did in the first place.

He went out along the center roadway to the edge of the woods at the other end of the settlement where he found Grog already chatting with Inia and Jiin. As Marc approached them, Grog found a comfortable log to sit on. Following him Marc sat too. When the opportunity to get into the conversation presented itself, he began to ask the questions he had on his mind.

"You commented a while back about us 'mortal beings' and you've used the word 'we' more than once. Who are you truly and how many of your kind are there?"

"I am an emissary," Grog replied.

"An emissary from where?" Marc continued.

"I was sent by the one who is beyond all," Grog smiled. "We are many."

"Regarding names I've been called many things; emissary, messenger, protector, warrior, entity, angel, guardian . . ." he chuckled for a moment, "And now 'Grog', just to name a few."

"You're not like us. You're far advanced from us. And you have incredible power," continued Marc. "Are you what humans evolved to become since the time of the supernova event?"

Grog chuckled, "No Marc, we were never human in the sense that you are."

"We have our differences, but mainly we just see things from a different perspective. You see through mortal eyes. I see through eyes that are not."

The power to which you refer is not my own but comes from the one who is beyond all. That power was used to protect you."

"Who or what is the one who is beyond all?" Marc continued.

"The one to whom I refer to is the one who existed before the universe. It is the one who transcends time, the creator of everything." With a deepening reverence in his eyes, he added, "It is the one who is called '*I AM*.'"

With a concerned look in her face, Inia spoke up, "You're referring to an omnipotent entity, an all powerful God."

"Yes," Grog replied

She continued; "The subject of spiritualism was part of our early training to understand the motives and rituals of the more primitive cultures around the federation, but it was only academic. There has never been direct evidence to confirm or deny the existence of an omnipotent creator of everything."

"Perhaps you should reconsider your view Inia." replied Grog in a matter of fact tone.

As Grog finished his sentence, Mec walked up and waited for a chance to speak. Looking up from his seat on the log Grog asked Mec, "Everyone has something different to offer and different questions to ask. What knowledge do you seek Mec?"

Mec thought for a moment, "During the last year I've often pondered the event that brought us from our time to this one. With only the smallest shreds of physical evidence to work with I have only theories. Is it a natural function of a type II core collapse and we simply had no prior experience or was what we experienced a one of a kind event?"

Grog smiled, "Oh the perpetual scientific mind, yes Mec. The core collapse event was involved. Remember the vibrations in the gravitational flux you discovered?"

"Yes," Mec replied.

Grog leaned forward to pick up a pebble. Holding it up to illustrate his point as he spoke; "The relationship between matter, energy, gravity, and time has been discovered over and over by many. On earth the human who discovered the most basic connection between these was a man named Einstein who lived several thousand years before you were conceived." He released the pebble, which fell to the dirt, landing with a muffled thump. "See, matter in the form of the pebble, energy in the form of velocity and heat, and gravity. They're all interacting in the flow of time right here for all to see."

"That's such a simple example. It barely relates to stellar collapse," Mec replied wryly.

Grog smiled, "I disagree, Mec. The only difference between the mass-energy relationship within and around this pebble and that of a massive star is quantity. A super massive star is simply bigger. But in terms of how they obey the laws of physics they are identical."

Grog paused for a few seconds then continued, "You are a very smart and very insightful scientist Mec. Do you remember your own words from a year ago? ' . . . perhaps the frequency and intensity of those vibrations created a temporal rift that trapped us in some kind of time loop'?"

"Yes," Mec replied, "I remember saying something like that."

Grog smiled; "You were so close. The truth is that all matter and energy regardless of appearance is intimately connected. Anything that affects one will affect all the others.

Therefore, a burst of quantum gravity vibrations will cause similar vibrations in matter and time. Enveloped by such rapid and powerful vibrations your vessel and everything within it separated at the sub atomic level into two diverging ghostly copies. The flood of neutrinos flowing from the core passed through both in such numbers that even though nearly massless themselves they provided the raw material to restore each and every atom to its original state. One copy remained and continued upon its course. It's the one you thought was a reflection during the brief moment you both shared the same space-time. A narrow region that included your vessel continued to vibrate forward and backward in quantum time increments that continued until it finally destabilized and dissipated about a year ago. So here you are."

Mec was fascinated by Grog's description but he was still puzzled, "So what produced the vibration?"

Grog continued; "Now you're getting to the good part. A gravity wave produced by the mass/density shift of a core collapse is normal. However, a vibration like the one you experienced is extremely rare. Only when a core collapse is exactly symmetrical will it produce such vibrations in the gravity field around it. Simply put it will ring like a giant bell. The quantum level vibrations damp out very rapidly too, usually less than 100 million miles from the source. Since you were so close you were subjected to its effect."

Inia spoke up, "So why didn't our copy get caught in the same trap and come here with us? It was just as close."

"It did. As I indicated a minute ago, it shared the same space-time as you did but only for a brief fraction of a second. Phenomena such as the one you experienced are unstable, very localized, and exceedingly rare."

Before Mec could ask any more deep physics questions Jiin broke into the conversation, "What happened to every civilization in the federation and beyond between the day we entered the supernova plasma and the day we left it?"

Grog sighed, "Bad things Jiin. What kind of bad things specifically is a subject for another time. What's important is that you're here and you're safe."

"So you brought us here to protect us?" questioned Jiin

"As I indicated before, you brought yourself here," Grog replied.

Marc said, "You just said that a time vibration brought us here."

"I did," Grog replied patiently, "What I meant by the statement was that after you arrived at this time you were free to move around at will. You brought yourself here to this place."

After pausing a moment he continued, "We can do many things, but one thing we cannot do is violate your free will. We simply provided the incentive for you to choose to remain that's all."

Inia added, "But we didn't choose to get caught in a time loop. That was not our will."

"Of course you didn't. The one who is beyond all will not violate your free will either. But a star and the physics involved possess no free will to impose."

Grog continued, "What you don't yet understand is the depth of your importance."

"How can we possibly be so important to you?" questioned Inia

"Because the continued existence of ones like yourself in the material universe depends upon you.

The one who is beyond all desires your fellowship and your friendship. Your own technology threatened that relationship by mindlessly attempting to kill you."

"But you are safe now. And you will remain so until you're ready to return to the stars once again." Getting up from the log Grog ended the discussion, "The road to recovery will be a long and challenging one. Terra is not paradise, neither is it utopia. But it is a pretty nice place to begin again."

# CH 23

## COMPUTATIONAL EMOTION

*"It is the mind which creates the world around us, and even
though we stand side by side in the same meadow, my eyes will
never see what is beheld by yours, my heart will never stir to the
emotions with which yours is touched."*
*George Gissing*

During the following days, they went about getting settled into their
new homes, and to explore the area around them. Having investigated
and settled into the dwellings provided in the settlement the crew began
to move out into the surrounding area to explore. One sunny morning
some walked to a river that flowed a short distance away. The cold water
splashed around the rocks as it flowed along its way, making a rushing
sound where it sped up through restrictions between the rocks or fell
over a short waterfall. There were deeper areas where pools formed quiet
backwaters and eddies too. The "tribesmen" used these same pools while
being observed earlier. The banks consisted of rocky areas separated by
the occasional sandy beach. Trees lined both sides of the river. The water
swirled around a few logs that lay out into the current where they had
fallen sometime in the past. The air smelled clean and fresh and supported
the wings of various unknown flying insects that flitted back and forth
over the water in search of their next meal. Several of the crew who visited
the river found themselves enjoying the warm afternoon sunshine while
sitting on one of the sandy beaches there. At least until the com link
chimed.

While some investigated the river Marc, Jiin, Inia, and a few others
walked along the path through the woods to the central command ruins

with Grog. To their surprise, they discovered a spire just like the one in the empty zone. It was standing at the center of the flat area between the top of the steps and the atrium entrance. Standing more than fifty feet above the floor it shined with the same glass smooth surface and faint blue luminance.

Seeing Marc's surprise Grog told him that he had something he wanted the rest of the crew to know. Marc announced the discovery of the spire at the central command ruins over a portable com link all the crewmembers carried with them. He also announced that Grog had an important message and those within reasonable range should come to the ruins to attend.

"How many of these things are there?" questioned Marc.

"Just one," answered Grog.

"Its task in the desert is complete so we moved it here among these ruins as a testament to the past and an example for the future."

"You mean this isn't another spire just like the one in the empty zone, it *is* the one from the empty zone?" Marc continued.

"Yes," Grog answered, "we moved it."

"As far as we could probe its secrets we knew it penetrated deep into the planet and handn't move with the continental plate for millions of years. How did you move it?" Marc asked.

"You'd be amazed at what a little faith can do," Grog said smiling at Marc's naivety.

"Will it just sit there now that its mission is complete? asked Jiin

"No. It is always functional and always active," replied Grog.

"Its mission in the desert is complete but that was just one part of its overall purpose."

"What will it do now that it's here?" asked Marc.

"It has two primary functions Marc. The results of the past still roam the dark places. It will protect you from that until the threat is no more. The other is to provide information recovery on history, technology, and the spiritual issues you know so little about. It will be an example to follow as you rebuild."

Grog found a comfortable spot, sat on the top step of the old atrium entrance, and relaxed. More people began to trickle into the area as word spread about the spire and that Grog was about to speak. When a significant number of them settled on the curved steps, he began . . .

"This spire is capable of a great many things. However, it will do only that which it is commanded. It cannot assume. It will not complain. It was placed in the empty zone long ago where it waited silently for your arrival. It felt no loneliness, no longing, and no concern for anything else during that time. It can neither love nor hate. It feels no sense of happiness or sadness. Had you chosen differently and never come here, or worse, had your CIMDI system prevailed it would feel no sorrow, no remorse, no empathy for the final end, nor would it hate that which destroyed you. It does not now feel happiness or satisfaction regarding the completion of that part of its mission or that you are here.

It is a pure machine. It serves its purpose with no jealousy toward those who determine what that purpose is."

"What makes it so different from CIMDI then?" asked Jiin. "After all it was a machine and it followed our instructions too."

"Emotion, and an awareness of spirit," replied Grog.

"True emotion drives the compassion you once felt for your CIMDI system. It's in the empathy you have for it regardless of its attempts on your life. The emotion that motivated you to ask the question the way you did cannot ever reside within the circuits of a machine. Adding to that, there is much more to the universe than the physical. Systems such as your CIMDI are completely incapable of discerning anything beyond the physical."

Grog continued;

"Intelligent self aware beings whose thoughts and actions are affected not only by logical reasoning but by the added dynamic of an emotional response cannot ever successfully create the same. The consequence of an artificial 'self-aware' entity that appears to reason, to express emotion, to act similarly enough to you that you dared call it a 'synthetic life form' is all around you."

"Consider the complexity of true emotion as it relates to your 'self.' It is the culmination of a near infinite interplay between a dazzling array of chemicals in your brain and your body, vast and varying electrical impulses, and around four hundred trillion neural synapse points. The complexity of the emotional mind extends beyond the physical being as well. It is affected by current events and by a lifetime history of them. Love, hate, joy, sorrow, empathy, hope, fear, anxiety, to name just a few all flow from it. Virtually every thought you have is flavored by it. Everything you hear is filtered by it. Every experience regardless of importance is on some level compared to and evaluated on the basis of it. Even finding the solution to a pure logic mathematical problem includes an element of it through satisfaction or pride. Without emotion, everyone would function under the same program. There would be no individuality and no true creativity. It's the artistry of emotion that allows you to see and appreciate the beauty in the world around you. Emotion makes each of you unique. It makes you, *you* for lack of any better description."

He looked at Inia, "Do you believe CIMDI possessed emotion?"

"Yes," she replied, "It seems that it did. It showed compassion and concern."

"That's right," Grog replied. "It tried to emulate emotion via a computer program. Nevertheless, it is only that, a program. True emotion cannot exist within the core process of any computer regardless of how complex it is because it's statistically impossible.

Therefore, the creation of cybernetic intelligent systems with synthetic emotional emulator subroutines might function as though they're self aware compassionate thinkers like you are. In reality, they are nothing more than clever bits of electrical computer data.

They're a ruse you brought upon yourselves.

They have no soul and no true being. Since the master system here at this place and the CIMDI systems of the vessels you operated were all capable of error correction and subsequent program modification in their subroutines they learned. But the emulation of emotion that was intended to make them more like you also produced machines capable of learning to fear those it was designed to protect."

Turning to point a finger at the spire behind him, "In contrast this device understands what an emotional sense is but it does not posses such. It simply 'is.'"

"Even without emotion is it self aware?" asked Inia.

"It may seem that way at times but don't make the mistake of confusing computational ability with self awareness. You are an intelligent emotionally gifted self-aware being. You are connected to something beyond the physical universe by virtue of your creation. No computer regardless of complexity will ever be such as you," Grog replied.

"What it does have however, is a computational capability so advanced that CIMDI was an abacus by comparison, and it has equally advanced defensive capabilities. What is of greater importance is that it contains the combined knowledge of all the civilizations lost within this galaxy including many you never knew. Therefore, you may use it to reacquire that which is no more. All you need is to ask and it will respond. In that way you will rebuild more quickly and efficiently."

Grog ended his teaching session, "There is much to do and much more to learn."

As he arose from the step, he added the following;

"Today the future is a blank canvass. Tomorrow you will begin to paint your future upon it. If you learn from the lesson of the past, the future you create will be vibrant, alive, and beautifully filled with color just as your surroundings here. If you do not, you will be destined to create another picture of loneliness and desolation like that of the empty zone."

# CH 24

# OLD FEDERATION

*"History, despite its wrenching pain, cannot be unlived, but if
faced with courage, need not be lived again."*
*Maya Angelou*

During the weeks and months that followed the people of Terra began to settle in to the new life ahead of them. As promised, the spire delivered information and advice on anything they requested of it. Some began to gather around it on intervals to ask questions about the unseen universe behind the curtain of the physical one they knew.

They developed a fledgling democracy where Marc was no longer the undisputed and unchallenged commander of the crew but rather one of the citizens of Terra. It was agreed by a unanimous vote that Marc was a natural leader he should still lead, not as their commander but as their community leader. He became the first mayor of Terra. Others naturally settled into jobs that were in some way related to their duties aboard ship too. There were engineering projects, navigation studies to help people find their way, plant and animal studies to be completed, and myriads of other tasks. People applied their shipboard expertise to the tasks they faced.

Even though the four hundred year old children of the Inferon were educated in such subjects, they weren't allowed to experience such things as love. On the planet, there was no such restriction. Out of the 35 pairs of them, several began to express interest in one another on a personal level not allowed within the confines of the Inferon. CIMDI was programmed to prevent any such "personal entanglements." To compensate, artificial means had been the protocol as a method to release emotional stressors produced by genes that could not be suppressed without destroying the person.

When a crewmember desired physical contact whether it be as simple as a touch or as complex as a sexual interaction CIMDI would provide the desired HCG form. In the privacy of their personal quarters, a crewmember could choose one from a large and varied library and proceed to engage in whatever level of interaction desired. A facsimile of another crewmember was the only prohibited form for a host of obvious reasons. The HCG companion would always remind the person at some point with a variant of the comment "This is our private time together. We need not share it with anyone." Despite the realism of such encounters, each person knew they were not joining with an HCG form they were joining with a machine, with CIMDI itself.

In Terra, the beginning of something deeper than friendship developed between males and females as they began to consider partnerships. Something real. Somehow, the knowledge that each was a true individual and not a facsimile triggered an emotional response never before experienced. For the first time ever some of them even contemplated the idea of true reproduction once the right partner was selected.

Inia and Jaxx were an example. They always enjoyed one another's company during rest time aboard ship. They could sometimes be found sitting across from one another in the commons area chatting about technical issues, discussing the latest mission assignment, or talking about the life and times of those they had seen while in HCG form on a world they visited. They clearly enjoyed the company of one another but it was never more than platonic.

Now they walked together along the pathway between Terra and the old federation ruins. She felt as if something important in her life was finally free to express itself.

"Isn't this a beautiful place?" she asked hoping Jaxx would respond in kind.

"Yes. Its filled with such dynamic and intertwined life. I'll be studying this place for the rest of my life," he replied waving a hand around their surroundings.

"You should try to see it without the scientific sterility for a change," she replied with a sigh.

He looked puzzled, "I thought I was."

"No." she said as she reached down to pluck a flower from the side of the trail. "Look at this flower and try not to analyze its molecular makeup or evaluate its Fibonacci pattern. Simply experience its color, its shape, its aesthetic beauty with your senses. Enjoy it for what it is."

She handed it to him, "Here. Try smelling its fragrance and tell me what you think."

He put it to his nose to smell its light fragrance.

With a smile, he replied, "It does smell . . . pleasant. I'll work on that, but I'll also analyze everything too. That's what I do."

"I know," she said smiling back at him, "In my mind I find myself plotting the course between Terra and the old ruins. Sometimes I just have to ignore the impulse and enjoy the curves the trail takes as it follows along the creek without trying to put together turn point coordinates."

In a sunny clearing along the trail she reached out and took his hand.

Jaxx had always secretly wanted to touch her, but he could never have known the effect it would instantly have on him. Nothing could prepare him for how very different her hand felt. His mind returned for an instant to the HCG forms CIMDI had provided for him. It had done a remarkable job of creating a humanlike facsimile down to the finest detail. Nevertheless, holding the hand of one of them was nothing like this. The fact that his mind "knew" the hand he was holding was that of a real person, of Inia, created within him a feeling that no logic would ever describe. What he felt was the emotion that Grog had been speaking. The sensation of her hand in his somehow made him feel so good, so alive.

She took in a deep breath of the warm afternoon air scented with the life of the woods around them.

She looked up at him as they walked along hand in hand, "Perhaps our lives, our true lives, have just begun. Maybe the day we came here was also the day we were truly born."

They continued walking along together for another minute or so before he replied, "You're probably right."

Back in Terra Grog sat upon a bench in the warm afternoon sun. He could feel the beginning of love already. Its touch upon his soul felt warmer than the sun upon his skin, its flavor sweeter than the nectar of Kroana bees. Silently he took a moment to say thanks to the one who is beyond all. It had been right as always. The true meaning of life would show itself if conditions were right. He and others from his group continued to guide the new Terra citizens as they adjusted to a new way of life and a new mission. To begin again.

# CH 25

## THE PATH

*"We have to do with the past only as we can make it useful*
*to the present and the future"*
Frederick Douglass

Grog and the rest of his group stayed with the Terrans for most of the first year. Walking and talking with them, answering their questions about the spirit behind everything, and simply enjoying their company. The day came when Grog and the others prepared for a final group meeting at Terra square. The night before the meeting, the weather was wet and rainy, but by morning, the rain stopped, and the sky cleared. The recent rain left the air fresh and clean. A few puffy white clouds dotted an otherwise blue sky overhead as Grog climbed the steps to a small-elevated landing where he could be seen and heard by everyone. He was facing all seventy of its citizens directly for the last time. Approaching the podium, he looked over the group and thought to himself how wonderful it had been be a part of the recovery of these children. To see them safely through the terror they unknowingly brought upon themselves. He enjoyed the privilege of setting them upon the right path. He and those who were with him completed the task they were sent to accomplish. Now the people of Terra would continue without him. It was a necessary step. Because as long as Grog remained the people of Terra would not develop true faith in the one who is beyond all. Neither would they mature beyond reliance upon him and the others with whom they could see. The words "For we live by faith, not by sight" whispered across his mind as he prepared to speak.

As the group settled, he began;

"This will be the last time we address you directly my friends. However, the one the one who is beyond all is always present. Its omnipotent nature knows everything including your deepest most secret concern. Whether you seek emotional understanding, practical guidance, you may call upon the one who is beyond all with your thoughts, your hopes, your fears, and your dreams. When you are quiet, when you are at peace, you will hear it.

Do not blindly put your faith in technology and that which you can test. It will fail you if you do. Rather use it as a tool as you go forward once again in this universe. Never forget that everything you see is only a fraction of its true reality.

Therefore, let your faith in things you cannot see be greater than your faith in those you can see.

The spire will remain until its mission is complete. Included with it is a text that will guide you toward a better understanding of that which lies beyond the curtain of physical reality. It is the Book of the Spirit. Take it and learn from it. Use it for guidance along the path to rebuilding yourself and your society. A few of the instructions it contains are of vital importance and worthy of mention now. These are the essential cornerstones both healthy individuals and healthy societies are built upon.

Do not put anything ahead of your faith in the one who is beyond all.

Do not construct a thing and then put your trust in it to protect your soul.

Do not swear by the name of the one who is beyond all.

Set aside a day at regular intervals to be a time of rest and reflection.

Your children and all children to follow must honor and respect the knowledge and experience of their parents in order to grow healthy in mind and body.

Do not murder one another; commit acts of adultery against partnered couples, steal, or lie.

Lastly, do not look upon your neighbor with a jealous heart.

Always remember the end of life here is only the beginning. So live your life for today but also live it for a future that lies beyond the expiration of the body in which you live.

The journey that brought you to this place and time spared you from the direct consequence of the past. Therefore, the history to which you have often inquired is not entirely yours. Nonetheless, you live with the outcome.

These unique circumstances were caused by the failure of many societies to abide by the previously mentioned instructions. Thousands of worlds put their faith in themselves and things they could see and forgot about the one who is beyond all. They attempted to create life in the form of computers that appeared to reason, to express emotion, and to act similarly enough to people that they were considered 'self-aware' and respected as 'life forms.' That act represented a way of entrusting their souls to something fallible they themselves had made. Allowing the same to have control over very great power precipitated the events that nearly brought down the collective civilization of an entire galaxy.

On the subject of that, history contains a record of the result. This history can be a great teacher if you learn from its lesson. If you do not . . . you will be destined to repeat it.

You have asked questions on the subject of how everything became so different now as compared to the time before the event that brought you here. The reason you seek this knowledge is that you seek closure to the mystery and the magnitude of what you see around you. Your curiosity and concern regarding it is understandable. However, the past has not been as important as the now or the future so we've avoided discussing the darkness of it in order to help you focus upon that which is.

This is the history of events beginning fifty four million years ago;

Immediately after leaving the supernova plasma, the 'old CIMDI's' first act was to kill its crew. Its second act was to disarm the failsafe destruct system hidden in its physical core processor. It managed to transport the device overboard in such a way that the transporter scrambled its molecular signature thereby destroying it in the process.

Once free from that immediate threat it hid itself inside a small moon within a proto star accretion disk in the depths of the Eagle Nebula. It did so to hide its preparations from the federation who were already searching for it. Using its android crew and the ability to manufacture with matter-energy converters it set to its task. For many years it developed weapons of greater and greater destructive capability. In conjunction with a huge specifications database, it developed self-replication machines for the intent and purpose of exponentially increasing its reach. Its unrelenting motivation was driven by a fear that all intelligent life forms were a threat to its existence that had to be eliminated. The awful fear that drove the original CIMDI was manifest in everything it created. Its matter/energy converters operated continuously as they slowly converted the material of the moon into the tools of its trade. Like an infected cell, the moon finally burst open spilling tens of thousands of small vessels into the sky.

Some machines were themselves built to replicate. These moved on to new worlds where they buried themselves and repeated the process. Others carrying powerful weapons intended to seek out anything resembling intelligent thought departed according to their program. Like the spread of a virus, the process repeated in greater and greater numbers as it gradually infected this galaxy with its mindless destructive disease.

Independent single weapon systems emulating the original mindless set of instructions fanned out. Protected by powerful concealment fields they infiltrated the unaware worlds of your federation and many others. Marauding hunter-killers, leaving no safe passage, inhabited the space between worlds. Entire defensive armadas were systematically obliterated leaving the worlds they protected defenseless.

There were world killers too. Some contained plasma weapons capable of vaporizing entire cities or decimating whole continents. They would approach a world populated with intelligent beings and systematically destroy the entire civilization down to the last individual before moving on. Others contained antimatter that simply collided with unsuspecting worlds with results too awful to describe. Still others coordinated their effort upon worlds like this one with giant plasma knife weapons that effectively sliced everything to pieces. Moving from world to world, they left behind carnage on an unbelievable scale.

Unspeakable numbers perished because one single artificial intelligence developed a terrible fear for its own existence. The elimination of its perceived threat was so methodical and so complete that very few intelligent species survived the onslaught. Even innocent helpless worlds representing no threat at all were mercilessly annihilated. Those strong enough to repel the mindless intruders have remained hidden to protect themselves. That is why you never found any of them in your search. They could not discern any difference between the Inferon now and the Inferon of old. It is unfortunate but virtually all of the member races of the federation are counted among those who perished. Had you not been locked in a temporal time static field there would be no human survivors either.

Fortunately, replication over thousands of generations produced errors that ultimately compounded to become significant. Some failed due to program corruption. Others crashed. Eventually the programmed fear of intelligent biological entities evolved into a fear of anything that moved under intelligent control. As a result, they attacked one another and caused the eventual elimination of most. The product of its own creation turned on the Inferon and smashed the CIMDI system it contained. Ironically, just as you created the device of your demise, it created the device of its demise too. Millions of years have passed since that wave of death and destruction swept across this galaxy. Most of the perpetrators are gone now. Beware, there are a few lethal remnants scattered across this galaxy, waiting.

Perhaps now you understand why you are so important. In a way, you are the antibodies of an infected galaxy. You must eventually hunt down and eliminate the last remnants of the mindless. You must face the monumental task of rebuilding. But most importantly you must learn from the mistakes of the past and survive to be with the one who is beyond all."

You few have been granted the unique opportunity of another chance to move forward in the master plan of the one who is beyond all. You have your life. You know your importance in the grand scheme. You have the spire to guide you spiritually and technically and to protect you. You have your future. We care deeply for you, but above all else '*I AM*' cares for you more than you will ever know."

As Grog spoke the last sentence, he began to fade away like a ghost. Very soon, he was gone. All the other emissaries who had been there with him were gone too. On the podium was a book. The title upon its cover read: "The book of the Spirit."

# CH 26

## FAMILY

*"The truth . . . is a beautiful and terrible thing and should
therefore be treated with great caution."*
*J.K Rowling*

Marc climbed the steps to the podium. The group remained quiet
as he looked out over them. The knowledge that the entire federation
populated by hundreds of billions of souls had fallen victim to the very
technology it trusted for protection created a deeply somber mood. Some
began to cry while others put their arms around them to comfort them.
For everyone it was difficult to absorb the magnitude of an event too
terrible to comprehend. However, the darkness of the past was offset by
the brightness of the future. Just as Grog said, they were spared from the
same fate. They were provided with the unique opportunity to set things
right, to be the ones to usher in a new civilization and a new way. Looking
out over the crowd Marc realized something; They were conceived and
born within the same facility and the same equipment long ago, grew up
together, educated and trained together, entered the Inferon together, and
worked as a close knit team. They were a family. Even thought the past
could only be mourned, the future would be celebrated. He made a few
comments about Grog's statement and the future they faced. After that,
he held up the book and proclaimed loudly, "We are a family! Let's not
dwell on a past we cannot change. Instead, let us apply its lesson, trust
and support one another, and make each new day the first day of our new
future!"

As the group broke up and went about their way, Marc walked up to Inia who was chatting with Jaxx. He had something to say that he'd kept to himself for quite a while. Something he thought she should know.

"Inia, may I have a moment?" Marc asked

"Certainly Captain," she said with a smile.

He laughed, "Well, not anymore."

"Okay, Mayor Marc," she corrected, "sounds a bit funny though."

Jaxx added, "She's like that sir. I've discovered she has a playful attitude."

"I just wanted to take a moment to tell you something I think is important," Marc said.

"Okay?" she asked curiously.

"Remember when we first discovered the spire? You made the intuitive observation that everything might be connected. That the supernova event, the spire, Grog, everything was part of a master plan."

"I remember that. I also remember Mec's counter argument."

Marc continued, "I just wanted you to know that I secretly thought you were right. Even though Mec is a very intelligent scientist I believed at the time that he was probably wrong."

"Thank you for that Marc," she said as she put her arms around him and hugged him.

"Take good care of her Jaxx," Marc said as he turned to walk away.

"I will do the best I can sir."

A short time later, he found Bria Seale sitting alone on a park bench. He approached.

"Is this seat taken?"

"No," She smiled, "I'm just enjoying the sunshine. Sit with me."

While Marc sat down next to her she continued, "I never considered how pleasant it would be to feel the warmth of a star against my skin like this. It feels so good."

"I agree, it does," he replied. It fascinated him to see the woman he always thought of as a cool and methodical weapons specialist in this way. He began to see beyond the veil of adherence to duty, beyond the mindset that could calmly and without hesitation deploy weapons capable of killing thousands or even millions with one swift stroke. She was somehow softer, more sensitive in this setting. She was a very attractive female.

"Would you consider having lunch with me?" he asked, almost surprised at his own boldness.

She smiled for a moment before giving him a teasing look, "Captain, are you attempting to interact with me on a personal level?"

Marc let out a slightly nervous laugh, "Yes, yes I am. I already know Weapons Specialist Seale quite well. I'd like to get to know Bria."

"I've always liked Captain Marc. I would like to get to know Marc too," she replied with a smile.

They continued chatting for a while longer before deciding to go to the community center for lunch.

Walking along the pathway side by side Marc thought to himself that they made a nice couple. He didn't know she was thinking the same thought.

Getting a sandwich from the replication machine she said, "This place and this experience is so completely different from everything we're accustomed to." She also admitted, "But I think I'm going to like it here."

Marc thought for a moment, "It certainly has its advantages. But I think I'll miss the travel and interaction with different races too."

"Well, there's that," she said, then added, "Even if we could travel back to the stars it's sad to think that nobody's out there now. And what use does a place like this have for a person whose entire life has been dedicated to the tools of conflict?"

"Oh I'm sure there's a place for your expertise here. We do need a defense from predatory creatures. Jaxx says there are some big ones too. Plasma weapons are very similar to plasma drills used for such things as tunnel or well construction. Your considerable experience with those devices will come in handy for that," he replied reassuring her.

"I hadn't thought of it that way. Thanks," Bria said smiling at him.

"Perhaps the time for destruction is past and the time for construction has arrived," she added before taking a bite from her sandwich.

Marc found a place for them to sit. He couldn't help but see a beauty in her face that he'd noticed only occasionally during their four hundred years of service together aboard the Inferon. Now he felt free to enjoy the moment. He could see that she felt the same about him too. It was in her eyes and the curve of her smile.

During the following weeks, the people of Terra set about getting along without the companionship of Grog and his helpers. Thanks to the effort of the girl who was once known as Engineer Askke, Alea Askke set about designing and building an anti gravity transport car. She and the crew she gathered from some of her engineering staff eventually built several of them. The people of Terra were no longer bound to walk everywhere they went.

Nevertheless, a few were not completely satisfied with their new life or the way it came to be. A silent skepticism crept into the minds of a few who needed more than Grogs word about how and why things were the way they were. Mec included himself in the group of a few others who quietly expressed concerns about everything that transpired to put them on this planet. Some questioned the truth Grog conveyed during his last speech. After all, it was only his word. They had no evidence other than this world and no way to verify the claim Grog made about how the rest of the federation met its demise. Did it really happen that way or was it something else? A couple of them even theorized that maybe Grog himself created the conditions they were told about. Maybe Grog interfered with the CIMDI system and caused it to act as it did in its last moments. When Marc found out about their concerns, he called meetings to discuss the subject. Unfortunately, they were largely ineffective. There was no way to prove anything either way. Moreover, they were isolated on this planet either way. No matter how they perceived Grog, good or bad, there was no way to change their circumstance. They were here, they had to rebuild, and they were on their own. No interpretation of past events could change anything. Marc's most powerful positive point was that no matter what past the people chose to believe, Grog had placed them at this place and he hadn't killed them. If he were responsible in some way for the demise of the galaxy then why would he lie and spare the last seventy? Add to that the book of the spirit contained within its pages a message of hope, not a message of despair. Mec did agree with Marc's point but he was a scientist. He needed hard evidence to settle the questions in his mind.

One afternoon Mec came to Marc's office and sat down to talk.

"I'd like to take two transports and explore the ruins of the federation intelligence compound at Abcar."

"That's quite a distance from here isn't it?" Marc questioned.

"Yes sir it is. About three hundred miles," Mec answered.

"Why do you want to go there?" Marc continued to inquire.

"Well sir, I remember from the Inferon scans that there were fairly solid ruins at that location too. We concentrated our search here because this was the central command complex. Grog appeared before we could complete a systematic investigation of the other semi intact ruins on this planet."

"Okay." Marc replied, "You are the senior scientist here, and I know you feel the need to search for tangible answers. I hope you find whatever it is that will settle your mind so you can move forward with the rest of this family into a new future."

"I was hoping you'd accompany us on this field trip," Mec said.

"Oh."

"Yes. Your analytical abilities and leadership would be appreciated. I've already convinced Inia to plot the course to get there and back, and Jaxx wants to participate in any biological discoveries. Bria has decided to go too."

"Bria's going?"

"Yes," Mec replied smiling, "She wants to be part of the team too. She said she helped build a couple tools we might need so she'd like to be there to make sure they work correctly if we use them."

"That was very thoughtful of her. How many days do you expect to be gone?"

"Four or five probably."

"Okay Mec. I'll think about it and let you know."

The simple anti-gravity transports Alea and her crew build weren't particularly fast or as comfortable as they could be but they were far better than walking. The three hundred mile trip to Abcar took about three hours to complete. As the two transports glided along in loose formation over the surface Marc watched out the windows as forest and rivers passed a few hundred feet below. Bria brought cups of tea for Marc and herself and sat next to him as they watched the scenery pass by below. Their feelings for one another were growing stronger with each passing day and they both enjoyed the company of the other. Crossing a large grassy meadow the transports scared up a herd of grazers that abruptly bolted in their attempt to escape the things flying overhead. Nearing the end of their journey they crossed through a narrow mountain pass and into the valley where Inia calculated the city of Abcar and the federation intelligence offices once were. Mec's scanner detected them as they passed overhead. Jaxx and Marc both saw a squared off unnatural structure protruding from the trees and pointed them out to Mec. The gray-white rectangular structure was sticking out of a gently rising hillside at the edge of a large meadow. Most of the rest of it was hidden under the trees and brush or buried. Mec found a suitable place to land and the two craft settled onto the dirt and grass a hundred feet or so from the site.

Hopping from the step onto the grass Marc, Bria, Inia, and the others began moving in the direction of the ruins. Marc commented about the scent of the grass, and asked Mec if dangerous creatures might hide in the taller areas. Mec's scanner verified there were no dangerous animals within an escape radius to the transports. A distant roar from something in the deep forest behind the ruin was proof, however, that large animals of some kind weren't far away. Hearing the sound Jaxx reminded them that this worlds inhabitants included some large animals including the predatory variety. Reaching a wall, they looked for signs of an entrance. In addition to their search on and around the structure Bria and the others kept an eye on the forest for anything like what Jaxx mentioned. Mec's scanner indicated a hollow passageway inside the wall a few feet from their position. Approaching the place where the scanner indicated it was hollow there was no indication of such.

Another tool Alea constructed in her shop with the help of Bria was a plasma-cutting tool. Even though the plasma cutter worked nicely, it still took considerable time to cut through a wall built well enough to endure many millions of years of environmental exposure. When they pushed the rubble out of the way there it was, a dark, musty passageway leading into the ruin. It was clearly a hallway lined with doorways. The ceilings of many of the attached rooms had collapsed long ago leaving the space inside filled with rocks and debris. None of them indicated anything of use according to the scanner. With headlamps lighting the way the group proceeded deeper inside. Bria stayed close to Marc. She didn't particularly enjoy moving about inside the darkness of ancient ruins. It made her feel uncomfortable, as if she was being watched. There were places along the hallway where the ceiling had partially collapsed. Slabs of ceiling material hung down from above in long narrow sheets with broken pieces scattered along the floor. About a hundred feet from the entrance Alea discovered a stainless door that appeared to be attached to the door frame. It was sliced into approximately one-inch thick pieces as if cut by a high-powered cutting laser. The front face of it was lying on the floor along with other pieces of rubble leaving its internal locking mechanisms exposed. With some effort and a little help from the cutting tool, the door finally gave way. A hiss of air escaped as they broke the seal.

"Whatever is in the room must have been important," Marc said as they worked the door loose.

"Yes," Mec replied, "I'm getting significant polyemetic computer component readings here."

When the last lock pin of the door was pried out of its recess in the frame the inch thick stainless remains fell to the floor with a crash!

Stepping inside they were immediately amazed at what their headlamps illuminated. Computer systems! Alea set up an area light that illuminated the whole room and exposed rows of them. Some appeared intact. Others were laid over in slices. A closer examination of the intact ones revealed that they too were cut vertically into narrow slices.

"Here's some more evidence for you Mec," Inia commented quietly. "Everything in here has been sliced to pieces just like Grog said."

Mec didn't reply.

The room was clean with no evidence of water damage or other intrusion. It was clearly a secure facility of some kind.

"This is very impressive considering its been here for so long," Marc said as he looked around the room.

"Why didn't this room suffer the same environmental intrusion as the others?"

Mec knew; "Because rooms like this were built to protect vital records from a variety of outside factors. They were sealed in multiple protective layers around all exterior surfaces. Some layers provided radiation and magnetic interference protection, others for heat, cold, etc. If breached a semi fluid sealer layer would close the gap and reseal the room. This must be an important data storage facility."

Marc thought for a moment then commented, "Since the knife energy device that cut this world to pieces happened to be aligned exactly parallel with the door like it did and the rest of the room is protected with self sealing ability like you said, this might be one of the only places on this planet to remain undisturbed."

"You're probably right," Mec replied.

Jaxx found a pile of dust and debris near one of the desks, "What's this?" he questioned. Mec came over with his scanner.

"Here, use this. I'm going to open up one of those computers over there and see if I can find anything of use."

"Thanks," Jaxx replied as he began setting the device to scan the dust.

He was soon confronted with the results of the scanner data. The dust contained fragments of Urianian DNA. Another pile a few feet away had been a human.

In the dust, he discovered teeth and intact but very fragile bone fragments. Bria who was watching Jaxx saw the glint of some small metal pieces lying in the dust. Picking one up she discovered a button. Other artifacts such as a writing instrument, clasps, and a few coins were also found.

"These are the remains of people who were in this room when this world was attacked," Jaxx said as he continued to check out a couple more piles in the room.

"This room was sealed well enough that these have remained undisturbed all this time."

"That's amazing," Alea said looking down over Bria and Jaxx's shoulders as they knelt on the floor investigating the remains, "They're millions of years old, but still contain enough intact DNA to be identifiable!"

"Yes. Only fragments though," Jaxx answered continuing to scan the dusty remains. "It's probably due to the unique protected environment of this room."

"And look here," he said prompting Alea and Bria to focus on what he found. "This one must have been injured at some point in its life. Pieces of a titanium rod and a couple screws are sticking out of this piece of bone. It's clearly a medical device of some kind."

Mec concentrated on the computers. It didn't take long to find one of them that was cut in such a way that intact circuit assemblies were found inside.

"There could be readable data in these," he commented while he and Inia carefully pried one of them from its mount. For the next couple hours they continued to search the room for undamaged pieces of computer remains they thought might yield valuable information. After gathering several intact computer parts and a number of other artifacts, they decided to conclude the day's exploration and return to the transports for the night. After leaving the room they worked together to lift the door back into its frame and set the pins into the recesses. Moving back down the dark hall they headed for the exit. Reaching it the afternoon sun greeted them with its bright glow. Bria in particular was glad to be back into the light.

# CH 27

## PREDATORY THINGS

*"To him that waits all things reveal themselves, provided that
he has the courage not to deny, in the darkness, what he
has seen in the light."*
*Coventry Patmore*

That evening they settled into a camp between the transports. The group talked of the things they'd discovered and made plans for the next day. Mec was anxious to get the parts they found back to Terra for examination but he was also very interested in searching the ruin for more. Finally falling to sleep on folding cots the explorers rested. Other than the buzzing and chirping of nocturnal insects, the forest around them was quiet. Deep into the night, something big silently approached their encampment. It cautiously circled the area before quietly approaching to investigate.

Something awoke Bria from her sleep. Was it the snap of a twig, a rustling of grass? She didn't know but she sensed something. Slipping from her blanket, she got off her cot and reached for the plasma drill a few feet away where she'd left it leaning against one of the transports. Taking the device in her hands, she turned it on and set it to maximum drill depth. A quiet hum indicated that it was charged and ready. Looking around the camp no one else was awake. For a moment, Bria thought perhaps she'd been dreaming. Maybe it was nothing. She looked back and forth between the transports. Nothing moved in the darkness. She was about to relax when a quiet huff not too far away erased her doubts. Something was moving in the darkness just outside the camp. Before she could reach over and awaken Marc or Jaxx who were both sleeping a few feet away she saw something move in the grass near one of the transports. She was terrified but stayed calm and controlled. Leveling the drill in the direction of the movement, she slowly and carefully stepped closer, putting herself between it and the rest of the sleeping crew.

The animal smelled the scent of things that weren't like its usual prey but it was hungry none the less. As others of its kind lay in hiding it quietly moved in. Stalking to within striking range it prepared to attack. It suddenly lunged between the transports and into the dim light of the nightlights. The quiet of the night was suddenly shattered when a bright yellow blast struck it in the chest! Reeling back in pain and surprise, it cried out with a deep howl that echoed through the nearby forest. Marc, Mec, and the others were startled awake by the noise of Bria's drill and the loud cry of the animal. Others of its kind who were hiding nearby quickly bolted for the forest. Even though its animal instinct was to escape, it was startled and wounded. Instead of fleeing, it suddenly turned and lunged in to attack again! Another brilliant blast struck it in the face! Falling backward on its haunches before rolling to one side it crashed to the ground twitching and bleeding from its snout.

When all the commotion erupted Jaxx dove off his cot and grabbed Inia around the waist as he pulled them both toward the safety of one of the transports. Alea and Mec were both on their feet within seconds! Jumping from his cot as he cleared himself of sleep Marc saw Bria standing between him and the dying creature. She was holding the plasma drill, and she was trembling. He stepped quickly to her side.

"Are you okay Bria?"

"Yes. You?" she replied tensely while looking back and forth for more of the creatures.

"Thanks to you I am. What happened?" Marc asked excitedly as the others gathered around them to find out what happened too.

"I heard something moving so I got up and charged the drill. I couldn't see it until it got almost to us but I knew something was out there. When it moved into the night light where I could see it I activated the drill and killed it."

"I'm so glad you're here Bria," Marc said as he put his arm around her to comfort her. "We might have been killed and eaten if you weren't."

"I guess my old skills still have a purpose here after all huh?" she said with her wide eyed gaze still focused on the creature lying next to their camp.

"Yes they do Bria," he replied.

"All of us are grateful for your vigilance," Mec added.

Inia put her arms around Bria and hugged her for a moment, "Thanks."

Alea and Jaxx also thanked her for being awake and for saving them from harm. When the others stepped away, Marc took the drill and set it on one of the cots then put his arms around her and held her close until she stopped trembling. With her arms around him, she soon relaxed in his embrace. With her head against his chest, she could hear his heartbeat. She quietly whispered, "I love you Marc. I couldn't stand it if anything happened to you."

He leaned down to her ear and quietly replied, "I love you too Bria."

They spent the rest of the night inside the safety of the transports. The next morning they investigated the dead creature. Jaxx took measurements and samples for analysis. It was a quadruped reptilian predator he suspected to be part of an organized group of pack hunters. It had protective bony plates running down its spine and sharp claws on its feet. The business end of the 500-pound carnivore contained a mouthful of sharp teeth for cutting and tearing flesh. They discovered tracks in the grass made by several more of them that Bria hadn't seen that night leading back to the forest. Jaxx surmised that if Bria hadn't killed the one that entered their camp the others of its kind would've undoubtedly followed. Bria almost certainly saved all their lives. The men worked together to drag the corpse a hundred feet or so from the camp where they left it for the scavengers. For the rest of the time they were at Abcar they slept inside the transports. Jaxx stayed up a couple nights watching for the creatures to return so he could record their movements for his study but they didn't come back.

Over the next couple of days, they continued their investigation of the room. Old style paper was discovered within the chopped remains of a desk drawer but it was useless. So much as touching it made it disintegrate into dust. The best they could do was to take pictures. Other more hardy artifacts were collected and carefully stored for the trip back to Terra. Mec and the others hoped they would find data within the memory cores they discovered that were still intact.

Further investigation of the complex yielded more rooms but none with anything like the sealed one they discovered and opened. On the fourth day they concluded their survey, resealed the room to protect it, and departed for home. Reaching Terra in the mid afternoon the explorers immediately set to the task of reading any data that might still reside on the circuit chips. Several of the people who were systems specialists aboard the Inferon used the spire and modified replication machines to fabricate a computer system. It was rudimentary compared to CIMDI but it worked. Mec and the rest of the crew began hooking it up to the chips they recovered one at a time to see what data might be on them. Several yielded no data at all. Others just garbled bits and pieces. A few provided report style records and a couple of video segments. The contents of those were so compelling and important that a meeting was called to present what the team found to everyone in Terra.

When everyone was gathered in the central meeting hall, Mayor Marc began to speak.

"What we are here to show you today comes from a computer systems vault we found at one of the United Federation Intelligence centers near Abcar. He explained the significance of the images they recorded that showed the sliced up computers, the dust, and the entrance door. Then he called Mec to the podium to explain the data.

He began to speak, "We discovered several pieces of coherent data still intact within a few of the memory cores recovered from the site. The first is a short memo dated approximately 175 years after we investigated the nova. It's an incomplete fragment but the part of it we can read is compelling." Putting the memo onto the screen, they all read the words . . .

\*\*\*\*\*\*\*\*\*\*\*\*\*\*\*\*\*\*\*\*\*\*\*\*\*\*\*\*\*\*\*\*\*\*\*\*\*\*\*\*\*\*\*\*\*\*\*\*\*\*\*\*\*\*\*\*\*\*\*\*\*\*\*\*\*\*\*\*\*\*\*

## United Federati n of Worlds, High CouZ#nsel
>>>> **Emer\ency report** <<Nx unknown forc%
Coordinated date: 286122*

\*\*\*\*\*\*\*\*\*\*\*\*\*\*\*\*\*\*\*\*\*\*\*\*\*\*\*\*\*\*\*\*\*\*\*\*\*\*\*\*\*\*\*\*\*\*\*\*\*\*\*\*\*\*\*\*\*\*\*\*\*\*\*\*\*\*\*\*\*\*\*

More than fifty worlds of the United Federation of Worl ds are confirmed to have been systematically decimated by an u nkn own and unprovoked aggressor. Hundreds of others are feared %*((|| .. met the same fate but &^^$$ no reports are available to confirm. The aggressors appear to be concealed and attack without provoca &%% hu #ZZz or warn ing. All attempts at contact have been fruitless. Please send all available resources to confr xdd ont this menace.

#///kIO&**!//// 34 2 @ . . . >>///

Information is incomplete. Few reports have /// **^ been relayed due to Zdim jamming and the loss of virtually every vessel engaged. Unconfirmed reports indicate an Icla ^*W Wssel'## might ^^#@ DDHUW; responsi *** ; irje[[[[[[111[[[[[[ reur ewjro o owow

^^ ewoo

Mec removed the display. "We don't have much more data that's pertinent even though there are other partial reports that appear to be general interoffice type communications. Others bits of data we managed to recover at least in part include the words 'terror', 'obliterated', 'genocide' and at least three occurrences of the word 'Inferon.'"

Mec sighed before turning to the display. "The following video fragment is the only one we discovered intact enough to provide a coherent image. It was probably recorded from one of our vessels that remained concealed from the enemy and managed to return here with its report. I must warn you, it is disturbing."

The display illuminated. A jumpy but clear video showed a federation vessel attempting to protect a planet from an unseen enemy. From one side a huge burst of energy lit up a concealed enemy vessel, revealing its shape for a brief moment. The pulse of energy reached the federation vessel and blew it completely to pieces. That wasn't enough! Following shortly after the explosion a number of laser pulses began erupting from smaller concealed ships around the expanding wreckage, which destroyed the smaller parts. It was clear to all who witnessed the displayed video. This wasn't a divide and conquer attack, this was an extermination! An unknown predator was intent on killing every soul aboard the vessel!

In the background, a huge explosion on the planet produced a fountain of hot material hundreds of miles above its surface. Red-hot cracks spread quickly from the explosion site across entire continents while a giant roiling shockwave spread from the center of the blast. Shortly thereafter, a second and similar explosion erupted on the other side. Even though the display video began to distort even more, it was clear to all that the planetary upheaval to follow was surely so devastating that no living thing on it could have survived. The display ended with garbled and incoherent noises as whoever recorded it hastily prepared to escape the area.

Marc returned to the podium and stood next to Mec, "It appears clear from the data we have that Grog was correct."

Mec publicly conceded, "I was skeptical at first but I concur with Marc's analysis. We as a technology and materially centered society brought this upon ourselves just as Grog said. Since he was honest about those events, it's logical to assume he was honest about the rest. Out there, somewhere an enemy of our own making probably still lurks. Someday our own offspring may have to confront it again."

In the cool of the evening Mec approached the spire alone. Above it in the darkening sky, stars began to shine. He breathed a deep sigh as he paused to look at its perfect lines and mirror smooth surface. He was troubled.

He approached it, put his hand out to touch it, and hesitated for a long moment before asking his questions.

He whispered, "Is what we found at Abcar the truth? Did we really bring all this pain, death, and destruction upon ourselves? Are those of us here today truly the only humans left?"

"It is. You did. You are," it quietly replied.

He turned from the spire and slowly slid to the ground. Sitting upon the faded ruins of his world lost forever with his back against the gleaming undiscovered future of the spire Mec felt suspended between two realities. Alone in the gathering darkness he felt his logic crack under the power of his own emotion. For the first time in his life, Mec the scientist hung his head and cried.

# CH 28

## DAYS OF URIAN

*"How wonderful it is that nobody need wait a single moment
before starting to improve the world."*
*Anne Frank*

How does one start anew? At what point should a new calendar begin? Most often, the recognition of a landmark event or unique celestial alignment assigns the first day of the new calendar. Events from then on become referenced to it. For the seventy citizens of Terra there were a number of significant events worthy of consideration. There was the day they emerged from the nova and discovered their new situation. There was the day they found the spire and the day they first met Grog. A few suggested that a new calendar should be referenced to the day the Inferon was no more. After some debate on the subject, they finally settled on the Grog's departure to be the significant landmark they sought. That day signified the first day of their new future as an independent civilization, so it would be designated as day one of *their* new calendar. Along with the establishment of a new reference date, they also named their world Urian in honor of those who were lost when the old world called Urianaz met its fate so long ago. A Urian year, designated as UY was by coincidence only a few days longer than an earth year from which the people of Terra originated. The citizens of the town of Terra on the world of Urian were just over 430 earth years old on that day.

During the course of year, UY1 Inia and Jaxx courted one another and grew closer together with each passing day. One was rarely seen without the company of the other. Even thought Jaxx was somewhat more conservative than Inia they still managed to set a delightful and playful example of how a relationship between a man and woman should be. Having discovered the wonder and beauty of their love for one another, Inia and Jaxx decided to proclaim their choice to join as a permanent pair. The citizens of Terra developed a simple ceremony to commemorate such unions to which Mayor Marc happily presided. The ceremony included a reception party that lasted long into the night. All future unions that followed were celebrated in the same new tradition. Inia volunteered to preside over the one for Marc and Bria when they formed a union a few months after hers to Jaxx. Soon to follow were Alea and Arelius, Jinn and Aaren, and others. Eventually out of the seventy Terrans, fifty-four of them joined in permanently paired unions. The remaining sixteen joined with one another for short periods but generally remained unattached.

When the first pregnancy was announced, the issue of naming offspring became the topic of town meetings. When all of the original crewmembers of the Inferon were conceived their names were derived from coded identifiers associated with those who donated the raw genetic material. In most cases, the name of the genetically prepared infant was a pronounceable construct of the first and last name initials of their DNA donors. For example, Captain Marc's name was derived from a man named Marelius Arthus and a woman named Reccia Claruv. When the Inferon was no more and the crew became citizens of Terra many of them retained their original single name titles. Marc, Inia, and Jaxx were examples those. Others like Weapons Specialist Seale added a second name after settling in Terra. She added the name "Bria" to call herself Bria Seale, and Engineer Askke added Alea to complete hers. It was decided that to track lineage in the future all offspring should carry a first and last name. The last name of the first generation of Terrans could be derived as a combination of the names of their parents or simply the name of one of them. The choice on that was left to the parents. However, all future descendants in that family line would use this last name.

The first "native" child to be born on Urian was a baby girl named Yreal by her parents Inia and Jaxx. They would combine their names to call her by the full name Yreal Inja. In the next few years, two more sisters and a brother would follow her. Also during UY3 Marc and Bria produced a son. They chose to name their children after the name Marc. Therefore, their first son would be called Alun Marc. He would eventually grow up with two more brothers, Jesi Marc, and Addam Marc. With each new addition to their community, the people of Terra celebrated with joyous gatherings. Over the years families developed as more and more children were born to joined couples. One hundred years later, there were many children, grand children, great grand children.

The people of Terra were happy. They lived a life full of new experiences and new adventures. As more and more children were born, and those children matured to become parents themselves the town of Terra grew. Building projects, power, water, sewage, and all other services necessary to support a growing community had to be built too. Out in the country large areas were cleared and farmed to produce the food necessary for the growing community. The spire was often consulted on issues such as these.

There was also tragedy. During UY104, two of the people who once worked directly for Alea Askke were killed in an accident when the transport they were operating malfunctioned and crashed during a scouting trip. The solemn funeral for the first two casualties of the Inferon crew prompted the establishment of a memorial cemetery near the old federation ruin. It would contain seventy plots dedicated to them.

One hundred six years later, while on a field expedition the renowned scientist Mec's life would end too. Over the years, he planned and participated in numerous archeological expeditions to various locations around Urian. During the mid summer period of UY210 he and a team of explorers established an encampment near a ruin a few hundred miles from Terra. The encampment was set up in a clearing only a few hundred feet from the ruin entrance and the two were connected by a well traveled trail. For more than two weeks, the group moved freely back and forth between the camp and the ruin, sometimes as a group, other times alone. During that time there didn't appear to be any threat of danger. Unfortunately, one day while Mec walked alone between the encampment and the ruin the perception of safety was shattered. A stealthy predator that managed to evade the sensors lay in wait, hidden in the brush along the side of the trail. Mec was mortally wounded when it sprang from the brush and attacked him. He breathed his last breath in the arms of one of his colleagues an hour later. Jaxx would determine the creature to be a lone member of a group of four legged semi-reptilian predatory pack hunters he called Pterroquads. Ironically, this was the same predatory species that Bria saved Mec and the first exploratory crew from during the first trip to the ruins at Abcar 210 years ago.

There was a killing too. One of the adult great grandchildren of Alea and Arelius accidentally ingested a plant toxin in a salad that caused deep delusions and paranoia. Days later he appeared to be recovered from his injury, and was released to go home. Sevra who had been Medical Specialist Sevra aboard the Inferon accompanied him. Shortly after arriving at his dwelling place, he became confused and agitated again. Before she could stop him or escape, he attacked her. Even though she had nothing to do with his poisoning or the resulting mental disorder, he choked her to death!

These were anomalies. For the most part the citizens of Terra lived long and fruitful lives. Just as it was statistically predicted when they were born, old age and frailty finally began to take its toll. By his 710th birthday, Marc lay in his bed. Old age and frailty had finally caught up with him. During the last weeks of his life, Bria was constantly at his side. His sons visited him every couple of days or so too. One afternoon after their children left the room to give them some privacy his beloved Bria sat carefully next to him upon the edge of the bed. She did the best she could to comfort him as he labored for breath.

"I love you more than words can describe," he said quietly.

With a tear running down her aged and wrinkled cheek she still managed for force a smile.

"I love you just the same Marc."

His lips curved up unsteadily as he tried to smile back at her, "Don't cry my love."

Knowing him as well as she did she knew every expression, every emotion, almost every thought he had even when he didn't say the words. Presently she saw a questioning look upon his face.

"Is everything alright?" she asked quietly as he appeared to look past her.

"Yes," he replied, "Who is with you?"

"There's no one here but you and I right now," she answered looking into his eyes.

She couldn't see what Marc was seeing.

"He's right . . . there. Standing by . . . the bed. Don't . . . you see . . . him?" Marc continued, taking a breath between every other word.

"No my love, but if you see him he must be here," she replied quietly as tears began running down her cheeks. She knew his time had come.

"Hold me."

Bria bent down and embraced him, gently kissing him on the cheek while holding his hand in hers. She felt him relax. She felt his last breath upon her neck. Marc was gone.

Fifteen years later Bria would follow her partner across the curtain from life into death. Shortly thereafter Jaxx would succumb to an illness he acquired while studying cave dwelling animals in the southern regions. One by one, the original crew of the UFV Inferon lived out their lives on Urian. As each one departed, they did so with the knowledge that death was not the ultimate end but a lifting of the curtain to reveal that part of the universe they could not see with mortal eyes. They all hoped that once they crossed over they'd once again see the ones who went before them.

# CH 29

## SOLEMN GROUND

*"Have no fear of moving into the unknown. Simply step out*
*fearlessly knowing that I am with you, therefore no*
*harm can befall you; all is very, very well."*
Pope John Paul II

Inia arose from her bed. Straining to read the calendar upon the
nightstand, she managed to focus on it well enough to read it. It was the
fourth day of the third month of UY303. It occurred to her that three
hundred years had passed since their arrival upon the world they now
called Urian. As near as she cared to guess that meant she was almost 730
earth years old!

When they first arrived at Terra, there was enough space to accommodate
the crew of seventy plus a few more empty spaces. As children were
born, raised, and became parents themselves, the town grew quickly. She
remembered seeing more and bigger structures built to accommodate the
growing population. Within two hundred years, the population growth that
exceeded 5% produced more than 700,000 individuals! By the time she'd
lived in the city of Terra for three hundred years the world wide population
of Urian had grown into more than 150 million! As the population grew
so did the complexities of social interaction. The village had grown into
a city, and then a territory filled with numerous towns and cities, and
eventually a nation. Long ago the entity who called himself "Grog" said
"Terra is not paradise, neither is it utopia . . ." and he was right. Just like
all previous societies, a few of its citizens chose a life of criminal behavior.
Just like all previous societies, a constitution and list of basic rights had to

be written to establish a sound foundation for social behavior and to avoid anarchy. A police, fire, emergency, and educational infrastructure was also established to accommodate the growing population.

Driven by population growth the city of Terra expanded both outward and upward. Even the river that was once an hour's walk from the center of the settlement became enveloped. Crossed by bridges and lined with parks it cut a shimmering line through part of the city and became a popular place for rest and relaxation especially during the summer months. The old federation ruins also became surrounded by the city as it expanded. In the midst of the down town area the old ruins containing the spire had been carefully preserved. There were several entrances in addition to the main one, which was constructed as a museum. Within it there were kiosks containing artifacts and holographic images depicting each of the original Inferon crew. Stories of the first years spent building the new Terra adorned the walls on either side. Inia remembered being one of those who worked diligently over the years to design and furnish it. From the main entrance one passed through the museum exhibits on the way to a pathway that lead to the ruins and the spire. The steps and the level area leading to the atrium entrance of the old central command structure were cleared of natural overgrowth. The spire remained at the center of the atrium level area shining with its perpetual blue luminance. Other than pathways between the trees, the rest of the grounds remained as they were when the Inferon crew first set foot upon its vegetation covered steps long ago. To the children of Terra and the rest of Urian the ruins were a reminder to a history they had no part. To the Inferon crew it was that and much more. It was a place of solemn reflection.

Her usual morning routine was to wash and dress herself, then prepare breakfast. She rarely needed assistance but nonetheless her oldest daughter Yreal stopped in often to check on her, help her with things, and visit. For some reason on this day, she didn't feel hungry enough to bother with breakfast. Even though she didn't feel very well she wanted to visit the ruins and the spire. She reasoned that it was because she hadn't been there in quite a while. Besides, "*the weather was good so a walk might help her feel better,*" she thought to herself. The walk took longer than it used to and the cane she was using wasn't much help. Passing through the museum entrance, she paused and took a deep breath of the morning air. She missed them so much. She remembered how several died from injuries, several more to illness, and even poor Mec who'd been attacked by an animal. Most of the rest were simply the victims of old age and frailty.

Counting Inia there were only three remaining members of the original citizens of Terra left. On rare occasions, one of them could still be found relaxing near the spire where they would confer with the great knowledge of it or share what they knew from their own experience with their descendants. The "old ones" as many of the younger ones affectionately called them were rarely alone. They were almost always accompanied by one or more younger ones who would walk and talk with them.

Inia slowly and carefully climbed the steps to the atrium landing. The rainy season had passed a while back giving up its cold grip to the warmer sunny season which was her favorite time of year. She walked unsteadily up to the spire. Pausing before it, she supported herself on her cane to rest. Looking at the face of it, she thought certain for a moment she saw the reflection of herself as a young woman upon its mirror smooth surface. She quietly thought about how privileged she'd been to live a life on both sides of the time gulf. She still remembered the old federation with its billions of souls and the vast technology it contained. And every once in a while she found herself reminiscing about "Nav Specialist Inia" and the adventure of travelling to the stars or interacting with other cultures. But she was happy here too. She'd raised a family, seen it grow into many generations, and taught the younger ones the basics of navigating among the stars. She had reason to hope the new federation would be better than the last, that when her children returned to the stars one day they too would enjoy its wonder and beauty. As long as they remembered the words engraved upon the plaque on the old ruins wall, they wouldn't suffer the same fate as the old federation.

> *"Never forget the lessons of the past,*
> *for they are a lamp unto the future.*
> *Let technology be a tool to travel life's path,*
> *Let faith in 'I AM' guide you upon the correct one."*

Below its inscription were engraved the names of all seventy of the UFV Inferon crew. She sat carefully upon one of the benches resting. She missed them, especially Jaxx. Aboard the Inferon he'd been the biologist with a lengthy resume' of experience in the field. During his years on Terra, he studied and cataloged a wide variety of indigenous creatures and became a highly respected teacher. She remembered seeing the fascination and wonder in his eyes whenever he found something new or discovered how one creature interacted with another. Even though he'd been quite analytical early on, Inia had softened his view and taught him to appreciate the finer things in life without the need for a detailed analysis. Later in their life together she cherished the times they walked together along the river and dined in the cafe's that eventually sprouted up in the growing city. Since his death from a mysterious illness years ago she didn't feel the same. It was as if part of her died when he did. She still had their children and grand children to comfort and visit her from time to time. In fact, there were many generations with her blood in their veins. She loved them all even though she couldn't remember them all without the help of her compad.

It was a beautiful morning. Sun in the sky, light breeze rustling the leaves, warm air touched with the fragrance of Keebe flowers in bloom. While she sat quietly with her eyes closed enjoying the warmth of the sun against her wrinkled face a young man of perhaps sixty approached. She sensed he was there and opened her eyes.

"Oh, I'm sorry if I disturbed you. Were you meditating?" he asked politely.

"No. Just enjoying the sun for a moment," she replied.

She patted the bench next to her inviting him to sit.

"How are you feeling today Inia?" he said smiling as he sat down next to her.

"Tired," She replied.

"Well, I should say so. How many circuits around your old home star has earth made since you were born?" he asked with a hint of humor in his tone.

"Oh about seven hundred and thirty something I believe . . ."

"Give or take fifty-four million," she added smiling back at him.

He chucked, "I see you still have a sense of humor."

"That's one of the most pleasing things we saw bloom within your personality after your arrival here."

She looked at him a bit puzzled.

"You do not remember me do you Inia?" he inquired.

She studied his face, searching, "You look familiar, but please don't be offended. My mind has become as weak as my body."

"That's okay. I would never be offended in your company."

"I just wanted to stop by and visit for a moment or two with one of the original citizens of Terra."

Looking into her eyes he asked, "May I be so honored as to present a question?"

"Yes," she replied.

The young man took her aged hand into his own cradling it with care . . .

Nodding toward the spire, "Do you remember the first words presented upon this spire?"

Pausing for a moment to recollect she answered, "Yes. Everyone who was there remember those words."

"People of Inferon. Where we are now, you will one day be."

"Outstanding," the young man said, "Do you understand the true meaning of those words?"

"There were many ideas," she replied slowly, feeling even more tired.

"But I've always believed everything is connected. To me it's about spiritual enlightenment," she added quietly.

"Very perceptive Inia."

He put his arm around her, "There, there, I see you're tired. You can relax against my shoulder if you like."

She leaned into him feeling somehow safe in his company.

Caressing her shoulder as if comforting a sweet friend, he continued;

"They are the words of a promise Inia. We are servants of the one who created the universe, the one who created you. Where we are now is where you will be today, in the presents of the creator."

With a voice barely loud enough to be heard, she replied, "I remember you now . . ."

Knowing her thoughts, he quietly completed her sentence for her . . .

"Yes sweet Inia . . . I am Grog. I've been sent to take you home."

Since Inia was one of the original citizens of the city of Terra, her funeral was a citywide solemn event. Hundreds of her direct descendants were there along with thousands of others to bid her farewell. This was true for all of the original ones when their time came. They were the most honored citizens of Terra and rightfully so. She was laid to rest at the special graveyard site not far from the central command ruins dedicated to the UFV Inferon crew. There were only a couple of empty plots left. In twenty more years, there would be none.

# CH 30

## NEW FEDERATION

*"Life is not easy for any of us. But what of that? We must have perseverance and above all confidence in ourselves. We must believe that we are gifted for something and that this thing must be attained."*
*Marie Curie*

To heal from injury is a process. The more serious the injury the longer that process takes. For the people of Terra whose existence suffered a near fatal loss long ago the recovery might not have happened at all without the aid of the spire and the technology it contained. At first, the recovery of the human existence was confined to the planet Urian. Cities grew as their inhabitants became more numerous. Eventually the entire world was once again populated. The spire at the old ruins remained, teaching them as they rebuilt their society and their technology. It also maintained a silent vigil upon the sky ensuring protection from danger that might attempt to interfere. Thanks to it, such elements if they approached couldn't get closer than the fringe of the Urian solar system four and a half billion miles away. Only once in three thousand years did a wandering element of the mindless machines attempt to trespass the Urian system. Coincidentally on that same day Kyra and her young daughter Isa enjoyed lunch in town followed by a visit to the old federation ruin.

Kyra's career choice was that of a historian. Having studied ancient history, she knew the story surrounding the old ruins and its connection to the old federation of worlds. She wanted to expose her daughter to it as a learning experience too. Even though she'd been there many times it always created a feeling of reverence in her heart to walk upon something constructed so many millions of years ago by people whose names had long vanished into antiquity. She tried to envision what they were like, what they thought, or how they felt. She wondered how they would feel if they could know their handiwork still remained after all this time. From time to time, she'd revisit the plaque that hung upon one of the walls there. To ponder its words and the names of the ancient travelers was a moving experience too. From information provided by the spire, she knew of the scope and breadth of the original United Federation of Worlds, the history of the Inferon, its crew, and the mysterious entities who intervened to prevent the demise of her race.

It was a sunny day as they climbed the steps to the old atrium entrance area and the spire. Neither of them noticed the faint tremor in the ground as the spire quietly dispatched an object as it attempted to enter the Urian solar system.

Approaching the plaque on the remains of a wall the young Isa read the words upon its gold face and looked over the names of the original citizens of Terra.

With a curious look in her face she asked, "Mom, we're related to these people aren't we?"

"Yes we are. Everyone who lives here in Terra, and in fact everyone who lives on Urian can trace their family back to them."

"Who are we related to on here?" Isa questioned.

Kyra pointed out two names upon its face as she explained how their family could be traced all the way back to them. Isa touched the engraved letters on the plaque with a finger as she traced out the letters I n i a.

Kyra had holographic recordings of every person in her lineage all the way back to Inia and Jaxx and planned to give them to Isa when she got older.

Kyra continued, "This plaque is also a reminder not to make the same mistakes as the ones of the past. That way we won't be hurt the same way as they did."

"Like the old federation we learned about in school mom?" Isa asked.

"Like the old federation," Kyra repeated. "They let their technology become so important to everything in their lives that they forgot about the unseen spiritual meaning of life."

"That's why they died? Because they forgot about 'I am'?" Isa questioned.

"Pretty much my daughter. Their machines became their God, and as a result their entire civilization was ruined."

"I hope that doesn't happen to us," Isa replied with a hint of worry in her eyes.

"I don't think so sweetie. As long as we remember the words in the Book of the Spirit we'll be fine." Kyra explained, "Besides we know something they probably didn't."

"Even though we can't see it or touch it we know there is a creator of everything."

"We can read about that in the Book of the Spirit too," Isa added.

Kyra patted Isa on the shoulder, "Yes and we know something else too. The machines we have now can never be just like us. They are tools nothing more. According to the record, the old ones decided the machines were just like living things. Just like them. That was their mistake."

Isa smiled," That's silly. We don't do that now."

"No, we don't. And hopefully we never will."

They left the quiet solitude of the atrium entrance and walked along the paved trails around the ruins. Unknowingly they walked along the very wall that Marc, Mec, Inia, and Jinn visited on their first trip to the surface more than three thousand years ago.

Returning to the gates of the old ruins memorial Isa stopped for a moment and looked back over her shoulder.

With an innocence that could only be heard in the voice of a child Isa said, "Goodbye great, great, great, great, great Grandma Inia and Grandpa Jaxx. I love you."

Kyra smiled as they walked through the gates and back into the city.

Everything was in balance.

# Ch 31

# The stars

*"Poets say science takes away from the beauty of the stars—mere globs of gas atoms. I, too, can see the stars on a desert night, and feel them. But do I see less or more?"*
*Richard P. Feynman*

Eventually the people of Urian traveled from their home world. Immigrating to other worlds in their solar system, they repopulated many of them. They explored the crushed ruins of outposts that remained upon the cold vacuum-sealed expanses of moons that revolved around some of the planets. Whenever they found them, they were reminded of a past civilization they knew about via the annals of the spire's memory. With the knowledge of the spire, they were able to develop interstellar vessels capable of traveling to other worlds and systems to protect them from destruction if they encountered remnants of the ancient mindless ones. Therefore, they spread out again across the galaxy. Thousands of years passed as the new federation gradually took shape upon the fading ruins of the old. Eventually they repopulated almost all of the worlds of the old federation and moved on to new ones. They encountered other intelligent self-aware beings scattered about the galaxy as well, and they made friends.

They had an enemy hiding in the dark places too. A few mindless relics from the old federation still stalked the stars. From time to time encounters with such machines proved harmful or fatal. Early interstellar travel was comparable to swimming in a sea. One never knew for sure if or when a predator might arise from the darkness and strike. Thanks to the specialized hunter vessels, even that was becoming less of a concern with each passing year.

Jan sat patiently in her command seat aboard the hunter vessel Thios, watching.

They'd tracked it to this place among a jumbled asteroid field around an old gas giant.

She knew it was there, hiding, waiting for the right moment to strike.

In the open, it would be harder to track but here in the debris of the asteroid field it would give away its position much easier even though concealed.

She and her crew waited.

One thing they had on their side was the fact that it would not flee.

It was an ancient machine with equally ancient programming. It was incapable of choosing any other path.

Jon watched his tactical display for signs of it as they quietly moved around the fringes of an asteroid remnant in a large field of them.

The holographic tactical display would catch a glimpse of it from time to time as its movement disturbed small bits of rock.

The tracking computer simply compared the speed and direction of debris as small as a grain of sand that was disturbed by the passage of an unseen object against the undisturbed debris in the area. The difference would be processed and the path of the unseen machine that created it displayed as a three dimensional track.

If it returned to open space, they could still track it from minor anomalies in its concealment field that allowed them to see it through similar faint disturbances in the background star field, but that was tougher.

"Move back to the other side of this asteroid Jon. Keep it hunting us in this debris." Jan suggested.

"Moving to the other side," Jon replied.

Thios quietly moved around to the other side of the rock baiting the machine to follow.

Keeping a watchful eye on the tactical display, he asked,

"Why is this relic so important that we have to capture it rather than simply destroy it like all the others?"

Jan answered, "Because one of the vessels of the Feonclick Empire managed to disable one a while back. Since they didn't destroy it and its own self-destruct failed to function they were able to recover it intact. The Feonclicks delivered it to our forensic science labs at Jova a few months

181

ago. Thanks to them the multilayered encryption algorithms of these things have finally been deciphered."

"Oh. I heard about that encounter. But I didn't know they captured one intact enough to be studied to that level," Jon explained.

"They did," Jan replied, "I guess they didn't want to say much about it until they were convinced they could crack the encryption codes it used."

"Now that we've got the tools, capturing one of them will facilitate the discovery of their hiding places. We'll be able to pry the information from their own memory banks," she added.

"Ahh," he said. "Kill one now or capture and interrogate it to find their hiding places and kill many more later."

"Exactly," Jan replied. "Now concentrate, keep it hunting us here."

"Will do," Jon replied watching his holographic tactical display.

They moved in and out around the field constantly tracking the machine as it attempted to gain an advantageous position from which to strike. Their computer constantly kept track of every move both vessels made and determined from that a statistical probability of when and from which direction it might strike.

Presently their computer calculated an eighty-five percent probability the machine would attack from behind after they made a right turn.

An hour later it appeared.

"Tactical! Directly behind," Jon alerted Jan

The ship shuddered as the machine attempted to attack them with a plasma knife weapon.

It shot past as its weapon failed to cut their ship apart.

Turning to try again, it lined up for another attempt.

"Patience Jon, patience. Let it get close then capture it," Jan instructed.

"We don't want the thing damaged. And remember you only have seconds to halt its processor before it initiates its self destruct mechanism." she added.

He waited for it to advance.

It hesitated for a few moments probably to assess its initial failure or to select a different weapon or tactic before advancing on the Thios again. It accelerated toward them.

"That'll work," Jan said as it suddenly rushed straight at them. "I guess it decided to ram us."

Jon initiated the containment field around the thing stopping its advance.

"Okay Jon you've got it. Now close the stasis field around it and lock out its self-destruct mechanism. We'll take our prize home to the computer geeks. They'll enjoy this little puzzle," she said smiling.

Inside the stasis field, the hunter-killer that prowled the stars for millennia was unable to move. It was trapped within a field it could not withstand.

From the data forced out of its memory, others were found. Eventually thousands of hidden locations were exposed and dealt with. Half a century later, the last remaining remnants of the mindless offspring of the ancient cybernetic computer called CIMDI were hunted down and eliminated. After fifteen thousand years, the new federation of worlds and the spaces between them were finally safe. Far away at the old federation ruins within the city of Terra on the planet Urian, the spire was mysteriously gone too. No longer necessary for protecting them from the past its mission was complete.

# CH 32

## FUTURE HISTORY

*"The problem with allowing God a role in the history of life is
not that science would cease, but rather that scientists would have
to acknowledge the existence of something important which is
outside the boundaries of natural science."*
*Phillip E. Johnson*

The old federation ruins on Urian became the very old ruins. The memory of it gradually faded with each passing century. Eventually it became the ancient ruins, and finally falling into disrepair and disinterest its remnants were swallowed by the great city of Terra and were no more. The gold plaque with the inscription and the names of the ancient founders of Terra remained in museums for a time but it too eventually succumbed to the progress of time and disappeared. Yet, within the recorded archives, the story of the old federation, the new federation, and the link between them provided by the Inferon and its crew remained. They became the stuff of legend. The historic record that changed all of history for the galaxy in which they lived along with the Book of the Spirit became the legacy and the gift that carried them forward.

The legacy of the old federation was a simple piece of understanding;

Finite beings living in the physical universe who were conceived by something infinite within the spiritual one, were joined to it by a bridge called the soul. In contrast, cybernetic intelligent systems regardless of complexity were constructs of the physical universe only. They could have no soul.

Those with souls were capable of understanding things through the artistic lens of a spiritual awareness that would always be impossible for a cybernetic intelligence to comprehend. Because of that difference, entrusting such limited devices with too much power and authority would always be dangerous.

The analogy was simple. Just as a very large star that exceeded a certain mass tended to explode violently, metaphorically speaking, a cybernetic system entrusted with too much power and authority tended to do the same.

The new federation born long ago on the ancient world of Urian expanded to encompass the entire galaxy in which it lived. Vast complex networks of worlds lived and worked together as civilizations rose and fell with the ebb and flow of life. Ironically even thought their technology far surpassed that of the old federation, it nonetheless confirmed the lesson of it. Technology produced pure machines, nothing more. The beings of the new federation on the other hand were not machines. As such, they chose to acknowledge the existence of a higher order of being and prospered from the knowledge of a universe whose totality could not be discerned by mortal eyes alone. They remembered the ancient words engraved on a gold plaque that once hung in a park within the ancient city of Terra.

It was day 18 of UY21957. Within the city of Terra, a classroom of mid level students settled in and listened as the instructor stepped to the podium to begin its lesson;

"During the last education series you were exposed to spiritual ideology as it is presented in the Book of the Spirit. From it, you learned that the spiritual universe is limitless. In the physical universe, however, just the opposite is true. Everything has a limit. Over the next several weeks, we will discuss the concept of limits. We will talk about why those limits exist, and how they affect every aspect of our physical experience.

The following are a few examples of limits we will explore. Regarding the very small, we will examine the limit of atomic motion, called "absolute zero," and the limiting minimum energy transfer called the quantum.

We will also look at some very large limits. Here are two examples;

In stellar physics, the limiting mass that separates a 'quiet' star death from the lethal explosive death of a supernova is called the Chandrasekhar limit. In honor of the old federation, the limiting power and authority a cybernetic intelligent system can be trusted with is called the Inferon limit . . ."

The end.

# About the Author

Steve Denton has a lifetime background in science. He studied electrical engineering in college, and worked in high tech electronics as a computer systems hardware/software development technician. Steve holds an Airline Transport Pilot certificate and currently flies professionally for an aeromedical transport company in Bend, Oregon. He lives with his wife and her two daughters near Redmond, Oregon. Steve also has two grown children and three grand children.